MindFall

by

Darryl Sollerh

MindFall

by

Darryl Sollerh

Copyright Darryl Sollerh 2015

Published by Del Oro Company

ISBN: 978-0-9897535-3-1

MINDFALL

Awakening, he feels the flutter of a wind buffeting his skin, tussling his hair.

Opening his eyes, he discovers the blue-hued glow of a dimming twilight.

Above him, a dark sky foments, gathering clouds for a fierce storm while all around him a vast Salt Flat stretches out into the shadows, silent and desolate.

How he got here, or why, he has no memory.

Only now does he realize he's naked, inexplicably curled up in the middle of this stark, bleak expanse like a child, abandoned to an alien world.

Confounded, he climbs to his feet and, leaning into the driving gusts to hold his ground, he peers out into the twilight, just able to make out the black ribbon of a distant mountain range riding the horizon.

But as he stares at it, straining to estimate distance, its crest seems to be moving, undulating ever so slightly.

A crack of thunder booms overhead, sending flashing forks of searing lightning into the charcoal twilight, and the mountain range soon reveals itself to be a monumental tidal wave, a thousand feet high and a thousand miles wide, rolling, rampaging inexorably across the plains, devouring the world.

He stares at it, terrified, frozen by its incomprehensible size and overwhelming force.

But then he starts to run, faster and faster, trying to escape its impossible power as it churns towards him, dwarfing him, a wave bigger than the world rising up behind him, obliterating all as it rushes to overtake him, to crush and annihilate him when...

Graham Lewis jolts awake to feel his heart pounding out of his chest.

He rolls onto his side, reeling, trying to calm himself by taking measured breaths.

He then reaches for his wife, Katie, and the reassuring warmth of her body. Feeling her, he finds his anchor, and holds fast, pulling himself back from the abyss.

As night gives way to dawn, she rolls over and cracks a drowsy eye and knowing smile:

Happy anniversary, baby.

Happy anniversary, honey.

As she slides further into his arms, Cha-Cha, their indefatigable Malamute, bounds in, utter mayhem on four paws, and leaps onto their bed, prompting Graham to yank the sheets over them in an attempt to escape her cold-nosed smooches:

Run for your lives, folks!

Later, Katie listens carefully to Br. Ananda, an East-Indian Monk gives a homily in their small parish church:

Are we these bodies? Are we these individual thoughts, feelings, lives, with their individual joys and sorrows? Or are we, rather, like waves on an infinite ocean, searching for the shores of our Creator, only to discover He is both the ocean and the shore.

Driving home later, Katie glances over to see Graham staring out the passenger window, stewing:

What?

He grimaces:

Why do we even go?

Go where?

To that service.

Katie shrugs:

I go. You go along.

He shrugs, counters:

So why do you go?

She gives him a look, but he persists:

No, really. Why? I don't get it.

Don't get what?

'He is both the ocean and the shore?'

So?

So a Master in Computer Science, a PhD in applied programming . . .

Your point?

It's just words, Katie. Just a bunch of flowery words.

Katie tries to take it in stride:

I think what Br. Ananda was trying to say was—

That he's lost the plot? Given up on all things rational?

Katie takes a moment, considering how to respond, then continues:

Ever consider that sometimes you might just be a little too rational?

Graham balks:

Too rational? How can anybody be too rational?

You'd be surprised.

Graham considers as he looks back out the window:

So you think I should be a little more irrational, is that it? Join the choir loony-bin? Well, you may have a point there, honey, cause if anybody's in charge of this world, it's definitely the loonies.

She takes a deep breath, getting her perspective back:

Feel like brunch?

I feel like...we need a vacation.

As Katie pokes at her eggs Florentine with a fork, Graham looks up from his omelet:

They make it too runny again?

Katie puts down the fork:

I'm sorry about these past few months, love. They've really been putting the pressure on me, and it sucks.

He sits back, trying to temper his response as they share a knowing, sober look. Graham then tries to lighten with:

Thought government work was supposed to be dull, predictable with regular hours.

She considers, almost bemused:

Not the secret kind.

As they get back to their brunch, Katie's mood eases:

Won't be much longer now, anyway. We're really close.

You and your assistant? Grown really close, have you?

He offers a tiny, pointed smile. She gives him a look.

Leo's been a huge help.

Leo's in love.

Before she can deny it, her cell phone rings. As she checks the caller's ID, she winces:

Yes, Leo?

Graham's eyes roll.

Classic.

That night, back at their home, their anniversary party is in full swing, crowding their living room with effervescent friends, old stories, laughter and champagne.

As Graham moves about with a bottle, refreshing everyone's glass, he comes to Judy and Bill, their oldest friends. Bill readies his glass for more of the bubbly liquid:

Don't mind if I do. Happy Anniversary, bro.

Thank you, sir.

Judy leans in so that Graham can hear her over the room's cheerful din:

So Graham, how are things in the world of computer systems design these days?

I should've gone into programming with Katie. Much sexier.

He smiles and moves on to refill more glasses as Katie introduces Brother Ananda to a couple nearby:

Brother Ananda married us.

Ananda, noting Graham is in earshot, grins mischievously:

But I was only doing my job.

Graham smirks:

I heard that!

God loves you, Graham.

Graham tosses back:

Good to know. And you be sure to bring him with you by next time he's in town.

Minutes later, Graham slips out into his backyard cradling a glass of Cabernet and a piece of paper, stealing a moment to go over his speech.

As he does, he hears ice clinking into a glass and looks around to discover Leo, an intense, wiry fellow in his forties, mixing himself a cocktail:

Leo?

Leo looks up glassy-eyed, as if returning from another dimension:

Ah. Graham. Care to join me? It's a smooth ride to who knows where.

Think I'll stick around here, thanks.

And by 'here', you mean what, exactly?

Graham smirks.

'Here' as in my back yard, Leo. Which just so happens to be right here next to my house.

Leo shrugs, absorbing Graham's dig:

Then it falls on me to inform you, my friend, that what you think of as 'here' is nothing more than a delusion of mind.

Graham endures:

That, and a mortgage.

Leo eyes him knowingly:

You'll see. And it'll be your wife who proves my point.

Leo raises a toast, downs his drink, and immediately starts mixing another as Graham looks on.

Speaking of my wife, Leo, given that you see more of Katie these days than I do, no more Sunday calls, all right? That's our time. Understand?

Leo seems to go into himself for a moment, but then offers a begrudging nod before throwing back another drink.

Graham, annoyed, turns to go back inside, but stumbles, spilling a drop of the Cabernet on his shirt, making a neat, round spot.

Crap!

As he tries to napkin it off, Bill leans out:

They're ready for you, dude.

Moments later, Graham, hiding the wine spot under a sports jacket, gives his brief speech to the attentive, if teasing, room:

I'll admit it: it did take me a little while to pop the question.

Katie balks:

Try forever, pal.

A round of laughter and catcalls puts Graham on the spot:

Because I was a fool, okay?! Man, tough room. But I will admit that I can, on the rarest of occasions, get a little lost in my head.

As more teasing quips chime in, Graham forges on, compelling the room to settle as he turns to Katie:

So in conclusion, thank you, love, for waiting so patiently for me to finally wake up and see the light!

To an eruption of cheers, Graham kisses Katie and then steps aside to make room for her as she steps forward to make her speech, only to quickly choke up:

...Damn it! I had this whole thing I wanted to say...Anyway, I love this man more each day. And I just want to say...oh for god's sakes!

Graham steps forward to kiss her again as more cheers and applause envelope them like warm, effervescent embrace.

Later, as the wee hours reveal the quiet beauties of night, Graham and Katie are in their Honda, driving.

With the party behind them, and a moonlit stretch of Pacific Coast Highway ahead, they are taking their anniversary drive along the coast, just as they took the night they fell in love.

As a crescent moon arcs above them, traversing an infinite universe of stars, back on earth a balmy summer breeze brushes over the dark ocean surf, shimmering here and there before blending into a black horizon.

Katie smiles:

I love this little tradtion of ours.

Graham pulls the Honda over and glides to a stop along the road's shoulder.

Katie has already climbed out and is on the curbside as he steps around from the highway side to join her.

They fold again into each others' arms and lean back against the Honda as on a backrest, taking in the midnight views – from the dark, rolling waves to the sparkling lights adorning the curve of the coastline.

Katie looks up at him:

I know it's been a hard lately. Mostly because of me. But it'll only be a little longer, I promise.

He eyes her and then pulls her close and they kiss.

We'll be okay. Just...like to get back to the way it was before all this.

Me, too.

They linger a few moments more, taking in the soft, rhythmic roll of the foaming surf and the feathery touch of a light breeze.

They then share a certain smile as Graham opens the Honda's passenger door.

As she climbs in, he moves back around to the driver's door where the headlights of an oncoming, speeding truck briefly blind him.

He raises his hand to shield his eyes from their glare.

The next thing he hears is the pin-prick ticking of a small clock in the dark. Graham stirs, still half asleep as the ticking continues. He gropes for his nightstand lamp, flips it on and looks over to see where Katie is but she gone.

He looks to the bathroom, but it's dark too.

Honey?

He then sees a scribbled note on her pillow and picks it up:

'See you soon, my love'.

Frustrated, he falls back onto his pillow and stares up at the ceiling, muttering:

You gotta be kidding me.

As he rides out a renewed wave of frustration, he hears a knock echo up from the front door downstairs.

Surprised, he sits up to listen.

A moment later, he hears another knock.

Warily descending the stairs, he crosses to the front door to spy through its peephole to see what looks to be a Federal agent, flanked by two junior agents, all in suits, with wires trailing from their left ears.

Mr. Lewis?

What do you want?

It's concerning your wife, sir.

Graham, concerned, cracks open his door:

What about her?

My name is agent Saunders, and I need you to come with me, sir.

Come with you where?

Mercy Hospital.

Katie's in the Hospital?

Minutes later, he finds himself being raced towards the shadowed city, leaving the slumbering world of the suburbs behind.

Now dressed in a coat and shoes, he looks to Saunders for an explanation:

You going to tell me why my wife's in the hospital?

My orders are to get you there, sir.

Disgusted, Graham looks out his window as the van rumbles over a dark, steel bridge, traversing a black river.

He gazes down at its opaque waters. His mind is full of growing fear as he worries about the possibilities.

Moments later, the van speeds through the quiet city streets and turns into Mercy Hospital's Emergency driveway, appearing all but abandoned at this witching hour.

Graham, flanked by Saunders and the agents, rushes into the lobby and angles for the reception desk.

Dr. Jarvis, a preppy looking thirties, looks up from a file, recognizes who this must be and steps forward to greet Graham:

Mr. Lewis? I'm Dr. Jarvis.

What's going on?

You mean you...don't know?

No!

Jarvis shoots Saunders a reproving look before replying:

Two hours ago, your wife was admitted to our E.R. in a state of catatonic shock.

Graham goes pale.

But I assure you that everything that can be done is being done.

Where is she?

7

She's in our Intensive Care Unit on the third floor, but what we need to know is . . .

But Graham's already on his way, hurrying to a nearby bank of elevators as Jarvis starts after him:

Mr. Lewis?

Graham pounds at the elevator's call button but then opts for the nearby stairs.

Jarvis tries to keep up:

Mr. Lewis?

Bounding up the stairwell, Graham bursts out onto the third floor and, following the directional signs, navigates his way to the ICU at the far end of a long hallway.

Just as he arrives at its secured entrance, a custodian is exiting. Graham holds the door for the Janitor and then enters.

Once inside, he searches the rooms for Katie, moving past patient after critical patient, to be suddenly halted by the gut-wrenching sight of Katie lying unconscious in a hospital bed, trailing a thicket of IV lines:

...Oh god. Oh god.

As he rushes forward, his knees nearly buckle:

Honey? I'm here. Can you hear me? Honey?

As he takes her hand, a staff nurse enters, alarmed:

Excuse me, sir, but I'm going to have to ask you to leave.

What happened?

The staff nurse digs in:

I'm sorry, sir, but visitors aren't allowed after hours.

I'm her husband, goddamnit; now what happened?

Just then, Jarvis arrives and quickly reassures the staff nurse:

It's all right. Thank you.

As she moves off, Graham turns to Jarvis:

Is there anybody here who can tell me what happened?

Actually, Mr. Lewis, we were hoping you could tell us.

Tell you what?

Jarvis explains:

We've been able to rule out physical trauma, as well as a wide range of toxins . . .

Poison?

Which is why we now think her condition is most likely the result of some sort of severe, emotional shock or trauma.

Graham stares at him, incredulous:

What?

Jarvis tries to frame his words:

What concerns us most, however, has been the steady decline in her vital signs over the past hour. So anything you can tell us at this point . . .

An alarm suddenly blares, prompting Jarvis to quickly check her pulse.

Graham looks on anxiously:

What's happening?

Jarvis, all business now, hits an emergency call button as Graham steps forward:

What's going on?

Jarvis whips his stethoscope into position:

Her pulse is racing.

Why?

I don't know.

The staff nurse arrives at the door:

Twenty cc's hydralazine, stat!

As the staff nurse hurries off, Jarvis starts checking Katie's pupils with a small light:

Mr. Lewis, if there's anything you can tell us, anything at all . . .

I wasn't with her when this happened.

Jarvis glances at him, confused.

She was at work!

Then contact her work. Anything they can tell as this point may be critical.

Graham feels as if he's about to implode:

I can't...contact her work.

Jarvis looks up again, even more confused:

I don't understand.

It's a government facility. They don't take calls.

The staff nurse hurries back in with a loaded syringe on a tray, which Jarvis immediately prepares and then injects into Katie.

They all hold their breath as the alarm continues to buzz, straining what's left of Graham's patience.

Isn't there anything else you can do?

Jarvis shakes his head:

Anything else might send her over the edge.

As more seconds tick by, Graham looks on helplessly while Jarvis checks and rechecks Katie's vitals...until the alarm suddenly stops.

The room goes silent, save for the steady beep of Katie's heart rate registering on the EKG by her bed.

As Graham takes a deep breath, Jarvis looks over:

At this point, knowing what caused her condition may be our only chance.

Chance of what?

Saving your wife's life, Mr. Lewis.

As Jarvis's words thunder through Graham, he digs out his phone:

Where can I find you?

I'll be here all night.

Graham slaps at his phone:

I'm not getting a signal!

They're blocked in here. Try outside.

Exiting the ICU, Graham strides up the long hallway, making his way back to the stairwell by the bank of elevators.

As he does, he can see an elevator car door open ahead, delivering a hospital orderly pulling a tall, teetering food-cart stacked with meal trays.

Graham then sees the custodian mopping the floor, backing his way into the orderly's path. But neither seems aware of the other.

Sensing an imminent collision, Graham calls out to warn them:

Hey!

But the orderly trips over the custodian's mop, and, grabbing at the food cart to break his fall, causes it to topple over and crash to the floor, jettisoning and splattering its food-laden meal trays out onto the hallway's newly polished floor.

Graham hurries forward, instinctively ready to help, but by the time he arrives the orderly and custodian are already helping each other up. So Graham moves on, navigating his way on to the stairwell.

Moments later, he steps out of the hospital's entrance into the night air to try his call again. This time it connects:

Come on, Leo. Pick up.

But he then hears: '*The person you are trying to reach is not available at this time…*'

Graham clicks off, bedeviled.

His mind scrambling now for answers, he looks around for agent Saunders and the black van, but there's no sign of them, either in the E.R. driveway where they pulled in, or the hospital parking lot across the street.

So he heads back into the lobby and strides back up to the Reception Desk to find a station nurse:

The men who I came in with; do you know where they went?
She shakes her head:
Sorry.
If you see them, would you tell them I'm looking for them?
Graham reverses pivot and marches back outside, crosses the street, and then heads into the hospital's parking lot to search for the van.

As he walks quickly around, feeling ever more pressed for time, he suddenly hears a furtive:
Graham!
Graham whips around to see Leo, ducking out from behind a small Toyota truck, looking paranoid.
Leo! My god, what happened?
You need to come with me, Graham!
Come with you where?
Now. Before it's too late.
What are you talking about?
Leo insists:
You need to come with me to the lab.
Leo tries to usher him into the truck, but Graham resists:
I ask you why, Leo.
I'll explain on the way, all right?
Leo moves quickly around to the driver's side and climbs in as Graham delays:
Wai-wai-wait! I'm not going anywhere until you tell me what happened!
Leo's face flares with frustration:
I don't know what happened!
You mean you weren't with her?
No. I was with her. I just wasn't...with her.
Graham scowls:
What the hell does that mean?
I can't explain it. But if you come with me --
A car starts up nearby, spooking Leo, who instantly drops down out of view, enraging Graham even more:
Goddamnit, Leo, I want to know what's going on now!
That's why I'm here. To take you there before it's gone.
Before what's 'gone'?
The lab, along with all of Katie's work! Not to mention any chance of knowing what happened to her!
Graham's ready to burst:
So help me, Leo . . .

Ya gotta trust me, Graham...Please?

Graham looks back at the hospital and then at Leo, desperate for answers. Then Leo tells him:

You have one hour.

Speeding up a mountainside highway into a forested highland, Leo pushes the truck's limits, whipping around blind turns, straddling steep cliffs, causing Graham to grip the armrest, increasingly concerned for their safety.

How much do you know Katie's work?

Nothing.

Leo knows better:

I need to know what you know, or I won't know where to begin.

Graham, still suspicious of Leo's motives, offers only:

All I know is that it's called Mindfall.

And?

And it has to do with mapping brain waves.

Leo shakes his head at how far behind Graham is:

We're way, waaaay past that. We can now not only decode them, but generate fully functioning A-REFS.

Graham looks over, not sure what any of that means.

Leo, seeing Graham doesn't seem to understand, continues:

Alternate Reality Emulation Fields. Do you understand what that means?

Graham's not sure if he does as they race around another blind turn, only to suddenly come upon a firestorm of flashing emergency vehicle lights.

Leo quickly brakes, slowing his truck down to a halting crawl as they pass a horrific crash scene, replete with two ambulances, a fire engine and two Highway Patrol cars.

From the looks of it, a passenger car, now crushed and mangled beyond recognition, apparently barreled head-on into the front grill of the lumber truck heading up the highway.

As paramedics feverishly work to resuscitate one of the obscured victims, a loud bang on the Toyota's hood startles their attention forward to an annoyed Highway Patrolman waving them on.

So Leo accelerates again, still affected by the accident's fury:

Where was I?

Graham, still craning to see the crash, offers:

Something about alternate fields?

Right. Alternate Emulation Fields. It means with Mindfall we can take all the thoughts, feelings and memories from a given mind, and download them, so to speak, into another. To the point where you wouldn't able to tell the difference between which was your reality field, and which was theirs.

Graham lokks over at Leo, filling with alarm:
You telling me Katie was in Mindfall when it happened?
Leo nods. Graham grimaces.
Lord god...
It was her idea. She wanted to know for herself what it was like.
Graham stares ahead, reeling:
So whose thoughts, feelings and memories did you download into her, Leo?
Leo hesitates.
Whose?
Yours. They were yours, Graham. She thought they'd be safe.

They arrive at the lab, nestled into a forested mountainside.

It looks more like a small, windowless office building than an Advanced Weapons Research Facility. But then, its mundane, forgettable appearance is the point of its design.

Leo pulls into the parking area and pulls to a stop.

Climbing from the truck, they make their way to the shuttered front doors where Leo slides a keycard and then types in a security code on a keypad.

Once verified, the front door clicks open and they enter.

The facility is dark and quiet, illumined only by dim security lights.

As they move through more security doors using Leo's keycard and codes, Graham notes various surveillance cameras offering external views of the facility's front, back, roof and parking area, including Leo's truck.

Graham takes it in, finally getting a look at what has been Katie's secret world for the past five years.

Leo then gains entry to the lab itself and they step into a confined, windowless chamber lined with computers, featuring at its center a pair of high tech reclining chairs, connected to wires and cables.

As Graham moves about, stepping over thickets of improvised electrical connections, Leo begins to power up Mindfall, typing in various instructions to enable its full capacities.

As he does, he sees Graham trying to make sense of the lab:
Not what you expected?
So where was she when it happened?

Leo points:

There. On one of those.

He indicates one of the tech reclining chairs, which prompts Graham's next question:

So how did she get 'in' to Mindfall?

Leo holds up a pair of what appear to be dark glasses, with mirror-like lenses and an attached earpiece.

With these.

He moves to Graham, angling to fit them onto Graham.

What are you doing?

It's the only way we can find out what happened to her.

'We'? And where will you be while I'm 'in'?

I'll be right here, looking after you.

You mean the way you looked after Katie?

Leo bites his tongue, trying to win Graham's confidence, yet well aware of the distrust between them:

I...cared for her too, okay? And if you knew how to operate any of this, I'd be the one to enter Mindfall. And I mean in a heartbeat.

They eye each other, finally coming to terms. Leo adds:

It will be your algorithms. Your reality field, Graham. ...Unless you can think of a better way to find out what happened to her?

Graham allows him to finish fitting the glasses. Leo then guides him onto the recliner, and has Graham lie back, explaining:

Since we're trying to find out what happened to her, I'm going to program her algorithms into Mindfall, so hopefully you'll experience what she experienced.

Only it will feel like it's happening to me?

Leo considers:

My guess is yes.

Meaning you haven't ever tried this before?

No.

Graham eyes him, starting to get a sense of the danger he may well be in as Leo checks his watch:

Jesus. We don't have much time.

Leo hurries back over to the lab's console as Graham lies back, unable to see much through the dark tech glasses.

So?

So I'm loading Katie's information:

A few seconds pass before Graham asks again:

So when do we start, Leo?

Any moment now.

Graham waits...finally:

Now, Leo?

No response.

Now? Have you started it yet? ...Leo?

Still no response.

So Graham sits up, pulls off the tech glasses to look around, only to discover that Leo's gone. Vanished. No sign of him anywhere. And the lab is silent, deserted.

Graham slides off the recliner, wary now, and perplexed.

An alarm suddenly blares to life.

So he pushes out of the lab into the dimly-lit deserted hallway, beginning to hear the thumping pulse of a chopper descending overhead.

He quickly runs to find a security camera, and sees a SWAT team storming the building's entrance via one camera, while another beams images of an assault team repelling from the chopper onto the facility's roof.

You goddamn sonofabitch, you set me up?

He hears a loud explosion, and looks back to see via the security monitor that the assault team has just blown open the entrance doors.

Goddamnit!

Graham quickly looks around again for an escape route, and rushes off towards the back of the facility.

As he moves through its dark hallways, he spots an Emergency Exit and charges for it as the thump-thump-thump of the chopper's rotors shake the building.

Entering the exit door, he moves down a short, dark hallway to find another door which he cautiously clicks open to see the outside of the facility, and the forest tree-line only a short distance away.

Checking if the coast's clear, he runs for the tree-line as the chopper's search light pans over the facility.

Graham has just made the tree-line as the glaring, white beam pans over the trees, scouring the grounds, while the red, gun-site lasers of the SWAT teams ray out like deadly needles into the darkness.

Picking his moment, Graham then charges up the wooded mountainside, scrambling against the slope to secure his footing, but soon disappearing into the trees and shadows of the night, escaping the facility.

An hour later, Graham is still hiking, making his wary way through the dark, highland forest, guided only by a crescent moon's pale light as he crests a peak to finally see a way back down to civilization, so he trudges on...

After another hour's hike, Graham, scuffed up, descends a last grade to arrive at a bus stop.

As he moves to take a welcome rest on its bench, a bus suddenly approaches out of the dark. Surprised, he hails it, and it slows to pick him up.

He boards, struggling to give the exact fare as the preoccupied driver waits impatiently. He then finally waves him on board.

As the bus accelerates again, Graham finds a seat. He is glad that there's only one other passenger on board, an old, ratty-looking woman in grimy clothes, her face hidden behind a pair of playful, dime-store sunglasses.

Graham settles in, drawing in a deep breath of momentary relief and then notes that the old woman is changing seats, taking up one directly across from his.

Graham tries to ignore her as well as the odor of piss and booze radiating off her, but she seems fixated on him, leaving him no choice but to finally inquire:

May I help you?

The woman sneers, toothless, as if punishing him for having tried to ignore her in the first place. But just as he turns away again, she demands:

If you're dreaming, and ya wake up in your dream, who's the dreamer, and what's the dream?

He looks away, hoping she'll give up, but she doesn't:

I asked ya a question.

Graham turns, trying to establish some boundaries:

For which I don't have an answer. All right?

Graham looks back out the window, checking the passing street signs to get his bearings as the woman continues to stare at him, hell-bent:

Why don't ya have answer? Too complicated for ya?

He looks back at her, realizing she's going to press him until he responds, so he says:

If it's my dream, then by definition, I'm the dreamer. All right? We done here?

As Graham tries to ignore her again, she continues, undaunted:

So what's your dream, dreamer...Or could your dream be that you're awake?

Graham's eyes roll:

Do you mind?

As Graham checks his watch, trying to figure his next move, the woman unexpectedly nods as if accepting his wish, but then she suddenly lunges across the aisle to grab hold of his collar, compelling a face to face:

Whoa, lady! Back off!

As he tries to push her away, she spits:

Those that have eyes, let them see!

She then rips off her dark glasses to reveal she has no eyes – only hollow, sunken sockets covered with shriveled skin.

Graham recoils, finally able to free himself from her grasp and push her back across the aisle to sink back into her seat.

A moment later, the bus bell dings, signaling Graham's stop, and he quickly makes his way off the bus, finding himself on the outskirts of the suburbs.

The bus rumbles off, trailing a toothless grin from the old woman, who cranes to watch after him before disappearing again into the night.

Graham, trying to shake off her effect, makes his way back into the suburbs, walking past rows of sleeping homes.

He takes out his phone and places a call on the way:

ICU, please...This Graham Lewis calling about my wife, Katie Lewis? Any changes in her condition?...I see. Thank you.

Entering his home, he finds it dark and quiet.

As he steps in, Cha-Cha, their furry Malamute, runs up wagging her tail:

So good to see you too, girl. Katie's going to be home soon, okay? Don't worry.

As he tries to comfort Cha-Cha, Graham's eyes flood with sudden tears, forcing him to take a moment to regain his composure.

Rallying again, he climbs the stairs back to their bedroom, sobering as he realizes it would be wise to hide any evidence he was at the lab tonight.

So he reverses course and heads back downstairs, and into the basement laundry room.

Descending the stairs, he finds his shirt from last night, but with no sign of any wine stain.

Confused but pressed for time, Graham strips off his soiled clothes and drops them into a washer, turns it on, and heads back upstairs.

As Graham quickly showers, hurrying to get back to the hospital, the dark outline of a man approaches the shower stall, casting a blurry silhouette as he edges closer and closer until he finally catches Graham's eye.

Graham pretends not to notice, allowing the intruder to come close enough to reach for the shower door handle, and when he does...

Graham charges from the shower stall, driving the man back, slamming and pinning him against the bathroom wall tile, only to hear:

Graham, it's me!

Graham moves back in shock when he realizes he has Leo in his grip:

What? You sonofabitch!

Graham slugs Leo, doubling him over:

Thought you could set me up, you little prick?

No!

All that bullshit about Mindfall.

It's not bull—

Graham slugs him again. Leo nearly vomits as he sinks to his knees. But Graham pulls him back up to dig an elbow into his larynx:

I want to know what's going on, and I want to know now!

...Can't breathe...

Graham finally relents and Leo gasps for air:

You've got three seconds. One, two...

You're 'in', damn it!

'In' what?

Leo looks at him as if he's stupid:

Mindfall!

So help me, Leo—

When you stopped responding, I had to come in after you!

Graham's rage surges:

You lying little piece of shit! You tried to set me up to cover whatever happened to Katie!

He slugs him again, for good measure. Leo wheezes, but continues:

You're in Mindfall, Graham. As we speak. Whether you like it or not.

So help me.

Why, if I was trying to set you up, would I come here now?

Graham shakes his head, amazed and disgusted by Leo's incomprehensible insistence:

If we are in Mindfall, like you say, then where's Katie? Oh wait, she's in the hospital, which is right where she was when you took me to the lab!

Leo looks down, nearly beaten:

You don't understand.

Graham slams him back into the wall:

Oh understand perfectly: all you wanted, all you needed, was to get my fingerprints in that lab, right!?

No!

Graham punches him again. Leo drops down, cowering, whimpering:

Please, you gotta believe me! We have to go back to the lab now!

Graham scoffs:

Right?

Would I be here now if I was trying to set you up?

Graham eyes him, calculating the angles.

Far as I'm concerned, you're either full of shit, or totally insane. But either way—

Graham, still wet, naked, yanks Leo up from the floor:

You're outta here!

But I'm telling you the truth!

And I'm telling you to stay the hell away from me and my wife. Understand?

A moment later, Graham throws Leo out the front door and slams it shut behind him. As he heads back upstairs, Leo pounds on the door:

You gotta believe me...Graham!

As Graham dresses, Leo's cries suddenly stop.

Graham moves to his bedroom window and peers down into his driveway.

It's empty, as if Leo had never even been there.

A minute later, Graham cracks open his front door, checks for Leo, then quickly moves to his Honda, climbs in and accelerates away:

To hell with him!

As he speeds back into the dark city, starting to be filled with paranoia, he checks his rear view in case he's being followed.

But he finds the highway quiet, so he refocuses on the dark city rising before him like black daggers into the night.

Soon he's crossing over the steel bridge and the black river again, heading into the city's center.

Finding more cars in the hospital's parking lot than earlier, he enters its lobby, navigating the sudden rush of patients and families to head for the stairwell.

Bounding up to the third floor, he again makes his way down the long hallway to the ICU.

He finds the door ajar and hurries in to find Katie looking worse, her eyes more sunken, her cheeks more gray.

He reaches down to caress her forehead, tearing up...

A moment later, Emily, black nurse in her a twenties, enters.
As she checks Katie's IV's, she looks over compassionately:
Mr. Lewis?
Graham nods.
Your wife's beautiful.
Thank you.
He extends his hand:
Graham.
Emily.
They shake.
So how is she?
About the same since I came on shift.
As Emily checks Katie's respirator hose, Graham checks his
watch. It's stopped, so he taps it and it starts ticking again:
What time do you have?
5:37am.
He has to think:
Sunday?
Emily smiles understandingly:
Monday.
Graham sobers, confused, as Emily leaves.
Minutes later, as Graham buys a coffee from a machine, trying to
fathom where Sunday went, he hears:
For a brain to function—
He turns, exasperated, to see Leo again:
*It has to assume that whatever world it finds itself in is the real
world. Or else, how would it function?*
Graham stares at him for an incredulous beat. Then:
Go. Away.
Graham moves past him, but Leo pursues:
This world you see, that's all around us; it isn't real, Graham.
Graham balks, smirking at the irony:
I see. But selling out a friend is?
Leo grimaces, pained by Graham's incomprehension:
*All this? It's an illusion. An emulation derived from your and
Katie's memories, thoughts and emotions. That's all. What's more, I
don't belong in here.*
Finally, we agree. Now get the hell away from me.
It's a delusion, Graham. All of it.
Graham turns one last time:

Good, because then that makes you a delusion, too . . . So long.

Graham steps out of the Hospital's front entrance into a new dawn, trying to think of what else he can do to help Katie, only to have Leo step out after him:

What the fuck, Leo?

But Leo's determined:

Look, if you believe you're being chased by a wolf, do you run? Of course you do. Why? Because you believe the wolf is real.

Graham feels another urge to hit Leo, but instead just spins on his heal and starts down the block, trying to distance himself.

As he navigates the increasingly trafficked city street, building into the morning rush hour, he hears:

But if you were to discover the wolf was a fantasy, or a dream, and not an actual wolf, what happens to the wolf?

Graham turns, plants a right cross and drops Leo.

Was that real enough for you, Leo?

Leo wipes the blood from his nose:

Only because our brains, now exposed to this reality field, think it's real.

Graham scoffs:

Well, apparently your nose believes it's real. Now for the last time, goodbye, Leo.

As Graham starts back towards the hospital, a Latino man, maybe thirty, dressed in hip-hop garb, steps up alongside him, matching Graham stride for stride:

Graham glances over:

Can I help you?

Graham Lewis?

Do I know you?

We need to talk.

Graham stops to confront him:

What about?

Just then, a white Aussie, a few years older, seems to arrive from nowhere to reveal a waistband gun:

How 'bout we all go for a little walkabout, eh, mate?

What is this?

Your lucky day.

Graham. Wait!

Leo, oblivious to what's going on, runs up, still trying to convince Graham it's all a dream until he sees the gun and blanches.

Glad you could make it, too, mate. The name's Seal, and you can call him Roan.

As passersby weave around them, Seal and Roan try to nod pleasantly as if all is well.

No sense in making a scene. So let's all just take it easy, shall we?

Seal then 'escorts' Graham as Roan positions himself to 'escort' Leo, and they redirect them back down the block, away from the hospital, as Seal seems to want to explain:

Your wife's in considerable danger, mate, and so are you.
Really?
Let's just say: everything you think you know is wrong.
But you know the truth, is that it?
I know more truth than you'll ever get from him.
And who's 'him'?
The Sysmin.

Graham sneers, filling with rage:

What 'Sysmin'?

For a computer systems designer, you telling me you never heard the term 'sysmin', used to describe a system's administrator?

Graham balks, even more incredulous:

What system administrator?

Seal suddenly senses trouble and turns to view the busy street behind them, apprehensive and then looks to Roan:

Think we may have some company.

The street looks normal to Leo and Graham, but Seal nevertheless signals Roan and they suddenly grab hold of Graham and Leo, wielding them as human shields.

In an instant, five average-looking citizens suddenly draw automatic weapons out from overcoats to take aim at Seal, Graham, Roan and Leo.

A street panic erupts. Pedestrians scream and scramble for cover as Seal presses his gun to Graham's throat, threatening to kill him as the Plainclothesmen advance, poised to fire...

Seal and Roan glance furtively about, trying to determine their best escape route.

Graham, sensing Seal's distraction, suddenly breaks free and starts running.

Now exposed, Seal and Roan are forced to make a run, fleeing down into a subway station as bullets fly in their wake.

Graham, as he is running away from the scene, glances over his shoulder to see a cadre of plainclothesmen charging after him, too, with Leo now only steps behind.

A frenetic foot-chase ensues as Graham and Leo weave through the busy sidewalks, trying to outrun their armed pursuit.

On the move, Graham glares back at Leo and yells:

Stop following me, Leo! You're making it easy for them.

Only reason I'm here is you! Who else am I gonna follow?

Graham takes a mistaken turn into a warehouse's loading bay, and ends up cornering them as the Plainclothesmen quickly arrive to block any possible exits, and quickly close in on Graham and Leo, tightening around them like a noose, guns drawn.

Graham and Leo, panting for breath, look around, desperate, but they're trapped, so they raise their hands, giving up.

Graham wakes to find himself curled up on a cement floor, feeling woozy as a military Interrogator in his fifties enters, flanked by two muscled guards:

Get up, Mr. Lewis

As Graham comes slowly to, Interrogator steps over and kicks him in the stomach:

I said: get up.

Graham climbs painfully to his feet, trying to get his bearings as the Interrogator continues:

Who you are?

Me? Who the hell are you?

Interrogator strikes Graham across the face with a small, metal cudgel, knocking him back to the floor.

As Graham rides out its sting, Interrogator kicks him again:

Get up.

Graham reacts slowly, so Interrogator kicks him yet again:

Get up!

So Graham climbs to his feet again, now with a bloodied, bruised cheek.

Interrogator holds up surveillance photos of Roan and Seal:

Recognize these men?

Should I?

Interrogator strikes Graham again with the cudgel, knocking him to his knees.

As Graham rides out the sharp pain, Interrogator leans in:

Let's try that again, shall we?

He yanks Graham back to his feet.

Now: tell me who contacted you first?

Graham stares at him, confused:

My name is Graham Lewis –

But Interrogator strikes him once more:

I have all night, Mr. Lewis.

You have nothing because you don't know what you're talking about!

Interrogator signals the two guards. They step forward and prop Graham up, positioning him for another blow. And just as Interrogator recoils to deliver it, they all hear:

Enough!

Interrogator halts, turns to see a sixties man in a comfortable, worn-in suede jacket and an open-collar shirt at the door – a man clearly long past needing a suit and tie to wield power:

That will be all, thank you.

Interrogator halts, immediately demurring.

The guards release Graham and exit with the Interrogator, as Graham crumples back down to his knees, shaken.

Graham Lewis, husband to Dr. Katie Lewis?

Graham looks up, bleeding, lost, as Joe offers him a handkerchief:

Would you come with me, please?

They move through a cement corridor lined by a series of windowless cells, akin to vaults, and then continue on to a large, secure door to finally exit the chamber, prompting Graham to inquire:

Just what is this place?

An excellent place to leave.

From the outside, it looks to be an abandoned warehouse. Nothing more.

Joe leads Graham to an idling, nondescript black van, manned by an agent driver.

Graham climbs into the back seat to find Leo, now sporting a swollen, black eye.

Graham just shakes his head as he slides in beside Leo:

This real enough for you?

Joe meanwhile climbs up in front, and the van pulls away.

Graham waits for an explanation. When it doesn't come he asks:

Mind telling us what the fuck's going on?

Joe smiles:

A whole lot of bad judgment, which is always the first casualty of war.

What war?

Joe smiles, bemused that he needs to explain it:

The war on Terror, Mr. Lewis, as if you hadn't noticed – except that every time there's a new threat, a lot of folks in my line of work seem to lose their ability to tell the good guys from the bad.

Graham winces, his patience long spent:

So what are you, FBI? CIA? NSA?

Joe smiles:

Those my choices?

Leo shoots a concerned look to Graham as Joe continues:

You can call me 'Joe'.

Graham's had it:

Okay, 'Joe', how about you take me to see my wife?

That's where I am taking you, Mr. Lewis.

Joe's van drops Graham and Leo off at the hospital's entrance. As they climb out, Joe calls to them:

I'll be in touch.

The van then pulls away and they watch after it, shaking their heads. Graham then looks to Leo:

Ever seen him before?

No. Which is why we need to get back to the Lab, so that we can—

Graham nearly hits Leo yet again:

So we can what, Leo? Frame me? Waste more time on your delusional fantasies?

Leo leans in with a grave expression and whispers:

So that we can get you out of Mindfall.

Graham steps back, utterly dumfounded by Leo's delusional fixations:

Jesus, do you need help.

You don't understand, Graham.

But Graham just shunts up a hand to indicate he doesn't want to hear any more from Leo:

You have to listen to me, Graham!

Inside the lobby, as Leo tries to catch up, Graham stops a security guard:

I don't what this guy to come with me, but he keeps trying to follow me.

As the security guard moves to stop and question Leo, Graham is able to escape back into the stairwell and make his way back to the third floor.

Graham enters to find Katie now on a respirator, and it staggers him.

He then reverses pivot and runs back out to find Emily at the nurse's station:

Why's my wife on that machine?

She was having trouble breathing so we had to intubate.

Does Dr. Jarvis know about this?

He signed the order.

Graham returns to Katie's room, and despite his best efforts to maintain his composure, he breaks down at her bedside, no longer able to hold back the tears, anguish and confusion storming through him:

Ah honey, please get better. Please.

As he passes by the nurse's station again, he stops to ask Emily:

Is Dr. Jarvis available?

Not just at the moment, but I'll have him call you as soon as possible.

As Graham absorbs this, he asks:

Is there anything I can do?

She smiles, recognizing Graham's deep need to do something, to somehow feel useful:

If you'd like to bring her tooth brush, or any other personal items she might like to have around when she wakes up?

Graham hears her words like a prayer:

And she will wake up, right?

We're doing everything we can so that she does.

As Graham drives home, he places several phone calls to friends, but reaches only answering machines...

Judy, Bill, it's Graham. I want you to know Katie's in the Hospital. She's...not in great shape right now. Anyway, I'll give you the details when we speak.

He then tries Br. Ananda:

Hello? It's Graham Lewis. Katie's in the hospital. It could be serious...I'll try you later.

He pulls into the driveway, parks, gets out, and goes into his dark, silent home.

Graham steps in to find the house dark and quiet, with no sign of Cha-Cha:

Cha-Cha ...Hey, girl?

As Graham fills Cha-Cha's food bowl, he calls to her again:

Cha-Cha?

Still no sign of her, so he goes in search, moving through his dark, eerie home:

Hey girl ...Cha-Cha?

He heads down the dark stairs to the laundry room and flips on the lights to look around, and finds his shirt from the party, only this time he can plainly see the wine stain.

As Graham stares at it, shaken, his phone rings:

Yes?

What happened to your wife was no 'accident', mate.

Graham instantly recognizes the accent:

Who the hell are you and what do you want?

Think of us as your wake-up call.

Graham then hears vehicles pulling into his driveway, and bounds back up the stairs.

He hurries to a living room window and peeks out to see two sets of headlights pulling into his driveway as Seal continues over the phone:

Long and short of it is, we need to talk, mate.

As Graham peers out at his driveway, now identifying paramilitary soldiers climbing from the vehicles, he spits into the phone:

Do not contact me again. Understand?

He clicks off and moves to the door, and then carefully peers out the peephole to see Joe, flanked by soldiers, stepping up to the door:

Mr. Lewis?

Graham considers what to do and then opens his door:

I'm afraid your wife's assistant has gone missing.

Leo?

A known terrorist group has claimed responsibility.

What?

Which is why I strongly urge you, Mr. Lewis, to enter my protective custody.

Graham eyes Joe warily before responding:

No thanks.

Joe sobers:

I can't protect you if you won't let me.

I understand. But my answer's no. Thank you.

As Graham moves to shut his front door, Joe reaches to stop him:

I'm not sure you fully grasp the situation, Mr. Lewis.

What I 'grasp', Joe, is that my wife is in the hospital for reasons unknown, and yet nobody, including you, whoever you are, seems to trust me enough to tell me anything.

Joe considers, then replies:

I might be able to shed some light on her condition, but you would need to accompany me to my office.

Graham grows wary again, so Joe offers:

After which, you have my word, I will take you wherever you want to go.

A moment later, Graham again finds himself in a government vehicle, this time a Humvee, racing back to the city.

As they rumble over the dark, steel bridge and black waters, Graham looks down into their opaque currents, wondering what Joe's hiding. And it prompts him to turn to Joe:

What exactly is your role in all this?

Joe shrugs:

My role is to protect your wife and her work -- and you, Mr. Lewis, if you will let me.

Unimpressed, Graham presses:

In other words, you work for the Defense Department?

Joe smiles softly, reflectively. So Graham continues:

So if you're not FBI, CIA or NSA, what are you?

Suffice it to say, I am in a position to help. But I can see you will need to understand a few things first.

Graham stares at him, tired of Joe's coy games:

How about you tell me who signs your checks, and I'll figure it out from there.

Who pays me is not your business, Mr. Lewis.

But my wife is yours?

...Yes.

They travel on in silence until they arrive at a tall, downtown building and drive into its underground parking structure.

Moments later, Graham and Joe take a private elevator up to his penthouse office suite.

Entering the empty rooms, Graham shoots a look to Joe, noting the commanding city views as Joe moves to retrieve a pair of the high-tech lab dark glasses from a lone cardboard box, which he then holds up for Graham's inspection:

Do you know what these are?

Graham turns, instantly recognizes them and is about to say something when he thinks better and shrugs:

No.

The future, Mr. Lewis, where, thanks to your wife, alternate reality fields will be available to all.

So what's the problem?

The 'problem' is that, as with all new technological breakthroughs, there's a steep downside to the technology your wife has made all too possible.

Which is?

Which is why, Mr. Lewis, there are any number of terrorist groups trying to get their hands on Mindfall, and, or for that matter, your wife.

Graham eyes him, waiting for more, so Joe continues:

Can you imagine any weapon more useful to the terrorists than to be able to instantly transfer all their most twisted, extremist views into the ready minds of their greenest recruit?

Graham regards Joe, wondering how much he can trust him:

Tell me something, Joe. Have you yourself ever experienced Mindfall?

More to the point, Mr. Lewis, have you? Because then perhaps your question would be: why are you not doing all you can to help me save your wife

?

Graham shakes his head.

You didn't answer my question.

Joe, unruffled, picks up a remote control:

Here are some facts beyond any question:

Joe clicks the remote, and up pops a 'mugshot' on a monitor screen of an Asian male in his forties:

Ever seen this man before?

Graham shakes his head.

His name's Ahn Li, leader of 'The Burning Sky,' the terrorist group that tried to kidnap Katie.

Graham shocks to attention:

Kidnap her? When?

Joe arches a surprised brow:

You didn't know?

Knew that somebody tried to kidnap her? No! When?

Mr. Lewis, that's how Katie was injured. She was trying to escape her would-be kidnappers, and that is how she ended up in a head collision with a lumber truck.

As Graham's jaw drops, his mind races with visions of the accident scene he and Leo passed on their way to the lab, which makes no sense because the paramedics were still administering CPR to the crash victims.

Where, where was the accident?

On the road up to the lab. Now do you see what your dealing with? Leo taken. Your wife nearly killed in a head-on collision with a truck?

Graham eyes him, confounded as he tries to prioritize what to do. First, he pulls out his phone and calls the ICU:

This is Graham Lewis. Is Dr. Jarvis in? It's urgent!...Dr. Jarvis? My wife was in a car accident! Yes, I'm coming!

Graham hangs up:

I need to go to the hospital.

Very well.

As they ride the elevator down into the subterranean garage, Joe receives a text message and sobers:

Your friend, Leo?

He's not my...what about him?

An hour ago The Burning Sky kidnapped him and apparently has now decapitated him.

Graham sobers:

Jesus.

As they walk to Joe's Humvee, accompanied by the agent driver, Graham's mind begins to fill with questions:

Why?

"Why" what, Mr. Lewis?

Why would they kidnap him?

Joe, misunderstanding Graham's question, replies:

My guess; so that they can turn their every operative into an expert bomb builder, or spread the gospel of their radical ideology to every follower, all with the click of a mouse.

Graham shakes his head:

No. I mean why Leo? Why kill him? Why not try to extract as much information from him as possible first?

Maybe they did.

Graham's not persuaded.

You believe that?

What I do "know", Mr. Lewis, is that they will clearly stop at nothing. That is why you need my protection.

No thanks.

Joe opens the Humvee's door, biding his time:

The hospital?

Home first, actually. I need to pick up a few things.

As the agent drives Graham and Joe back to Graham's home, crossing again over the dark steel bridge, Graham gazes down at the black river waters, shimmering now and again under the rising moon.

As he does, Joe eyes Graham:

I think you should reconsider, Mr. Lewis, and allow me to protect you.

Graham takes a moment, deciding whether to say what's really on his mind. Finally he mumbles:

There's something you should know.

And what's that?

It doesn't work.

Joe focuses:

What doesn't work?

Mindfall.

Joe's eyes narrow:

And how would you know that, Mr. Lewis?

Graham gives Joe a frank look:

Have you ever been 'in' Mindfall? 'Ever experienced it for yourself?

Joe waits, avoiding an answer, which Graham takes to mean he hasn't:

Sorry to burst your bubble.

As the Humvee drops Graham off outside his front door, Joe lowers a window:

Mr. Lewis?

Graham turns, already on his way inside:

The only bubble about to burst...is yours.

Graham watches as Joe's window lifts again as the Humvee drives off into the night.

Entering his home, Graham takes a moment to gather himself before moving to collect a few of Katie's belongings, including a tooth brush and a nightgown, only to have Cha-Cha trot up unexpectedly from behind:

Whoa, girl, you almost gave me a heart attack!

Cha-Cha presses into him, urging his affection, making him feel halfway normal, even if for only a moment.

We'll get through this, girl, okay?

Checking if there's anything else he can think to bring, he looks through Katie's drawer and finds a lab keycard buried in her undergarments, accompanied by a note with the word 'anniversary' scribbled on it.

As he eyes them, his phone rings:

Yes?

Oh thank god you're home!

Graham is stunned by the familiar timbre of Leo's voice:

Leo...?

They're coming for me. You gotta let me in!

Graham, confused, moves back downstairs to peer through his front door's peep hole, but finds no one there.

Where are you, Leo?

I'm at your door, damn it!

Graham opens his front door to find his entrance and driveway quiet:

Where?

Your front door! Please, they're coming!

Over the phone, Graham can hear Leo banging to get in.

So Graham reverses pivot and rushes back through his home to the back door, and swings it open. But no one's there, either, even as Leo screams over the phone:

Where are you, Graham?

Where are you, Leo?

They're coming! You gotta help me! Please, I beg you!

So Graham rushes back through the house to his front door, and out onto his entryway to find it still quiet and empty, despite Leo's cries for help over his phone:

Oh god, they're here. Please let me in!

I'm outside my front door, Leo!

No, please, don't!

Over the phone, Graham hears the sounds of a dire struggle:

Leo?

As the sounds of a struggle continue, punctuated by Leo's shrieking cries for help, Graham backs into his house and locks his door.

A moment later, the call goes dead.

Graham tries calling back, only to hear: '*the number you are trying to reach is no longer in service at this time*'.

What the...!

Graham quickly dials emergency:

Yes, I need to report a...

The operator waits for a moment and then asks:

Report a what, sir?

Graham realizes he doesn't know what to report, and clicks off, perplexed, and his heart pounds in his chest.

He then quickly gathers up Katie's things and heads for the front door, only to hear a gun click from the shadows.

Graham freezes as the source of the click makes itself known:

Sorry, mate, but it's the only way we could get you alone.

Graham turns slowly to see Seal, leveling a gun at him, emerging into the dim light of the entryway.

Now be a sport so I won't have to shoot ya, all right?

Roan steps out from the shadows as well, to blindfold Graham.

Moments later, they shove him into the back of their Sedan parked across the street and climb in after him.

Roan burns rubber away into the night, launching into a dizzying series of quick turns to ensure Graham can't retrace their route, as Seal matter-of-factly opines:

If you weren't so self-convinced of how things are – or should I say how you think things are – you might already have seen the truth, mate.

The Sedan finally comes to a stop, and Seal and Roan hustle Graham down into a huge, open construction pit.

They then guide him through a dark maze of underground tunnels and immense storm drains to locate an abandoned sewer-control station, converted for their temporary use as a hideout.

As they enter, Ahn Li turns stoically to greet them, indicating for Seal to remove Graham's hood.

As Graham's eyes blink back to life in the dim light, he notes that Ahn Li looks like his photo, but speaks by whispering into a small microphone, extending from his ear to just below his mouth, producing a dry, monotone voice:

Do you know who I am?

What do you want with me?

I want to help you save your wife.

Graham balks:

Save her from what?

Li seems puzzled:

From those who mean her harm, Mr. Lewis.

By which you mean who, exactly? Her nurses? Her docters?

Seal blurts out:

They all mean to kill her, mate. Sure as we're standing here.

Roan adds:

If you want her to live, you'll help us, bro.

You mean like you 'helped' Leo?

His captors exchange confused looks. Li asks:

You speak now of your wife's assistant?

You know what I'm speaking of!

Seal smirks:

He thinks we did something to Leo. Don't ya, mate?

Graham turns to him:

If Leo's all right, and you haven't done anything to him, where is
he?

He's disappeared, far as we know.

Did he.

Li considers:

Is Sysmin one who say we do something to Leo?

Leo told me! Just before you took him.

Seal's eyes roll:

You are sadly mistaken, my friend.

Li insists:

We no take anybody, Mr. Lewis.

You took me.

Only to help.

You call trying to kidnap her "help"? The only reason she's in a
hospital is because of you!

Roan counters:

We didn't try to kidnap your wife, man.

Bullshit.

Li eyes Graham carefully:

Have you ever try Mindfall, Mr. Lewis?

Yes. As a matter of fact. And I'll tell you exactly what I told all
those government guys: it doesn't work. Okay? It doesn't work. So how
about leave me and my wife the hell out of whatever you got going on.

Is this what Sysmin say?

Graham's ready to explode:

Who's Sysmin?

Seal sneers:

Ever hear the term "system administrator"?

I'm only systems designer, so yes, I think I've heard the term
before, including "Sysmin" for short.

Li moves close to Graham, eye to eye:

The man you know as "Joe" is the Sysmin.

The System administrator of what, for godsakes?

They all trade a look. Li then looks back at Graham.

Why, this one, Mr. Lewis.

This one what?

Seal can't help himself:

This system, mate. The one you're in -- we're all in. 'Least for the time being.

They can see Graham is buying a word of it. Roan shakes his head:

Don't think you're in a system, bro?

Seal balks, digusted:

No. Not him. He's too good for that.

But Li regards Graham with more compassion:

How can he know...when it seem so real? ...So real, Mr. Lewis. Which is why we must first, we must recognize the limits of this system.

As Seal and Roan sober, they hear a noise echo up from the tunnels.

Roan instantly moves to a panel of monitors and flips through the various security camera angles of the tunnels leading to this station, looking for an intruder.

Finding no signs of one, he indicates 'no' to Li. But Li isn't convinced:

Time to go.

Within moments, Graham, hooded again, finds himself seated in the back of the sedan next to Seal as Roan burns more rubber through the dark streets and now heavy rains.

Seal takes off Graham's blindfold.

As Graham rubs his eyes, he looks at Seal:

Was that really necessary?

No. But this is . . .

Seal reaches past Graham, opens the sedan's door and shoves Graham out of the moving sedan.

Graham tumbles onto the road, cracking his head on the pavement and rolling into the gutter as the Sedan speeds away.

As he lies there, unconscious, he begins to feel the flutter of a wind buffeting his skin, tussling his hair, and he wakes up, as if he were waking from a dream.

He opens his eyes, to see the blue-hued glow of a dimming twilight.

Above him, a dark sky foments with clouds while all around him, a vast, desolate Salt Flat stretches out in all directions.

Graham climbs to his feet, recognizing this Salt Flat of his dreams. And as he turns, filled with fear, he sees again the massive tidal wave riding the horizon, sweeping inexorably, inescapably over the open plains towards him, swallowing the world.

He starts to run, trying to flee, to escape it, but it's no use. He has nowhere to run to or hide as it bears down on him, overtaking and subsuming him into its rolling maelstrom, spinning him up into its suffocating waters as it drowns him into oblivion, until…

He gasps back to consciousness, choking on the street gutter overflow of rain water under a driving downpour, instinctively rolling towards the road's center, away from the gutter, where he's startled back to the present by the loud, honking blare of a city bus suddenly bearing down on him.

He is struggling to his feet as the bus brakes; it screeches right up to his nose.

Graham, shaken, exchanges an adrenalized look with the woman driver, who is also riding out of her own adrenaline rush.

Gathering her wits, she opens the bus door, almost as an apology, and Graham, accepting it, steps around to board.

Climbing up to the driver, he realizes he doesn't have any money to pay for the ride:

This one's on the house.
You going by the hospital?
Close enough.
Thanks.

As he takes a seat, the only rider on this route, the driver slowly accelerates again, conveying him through the quiet streets as he stares out at the night, reeling, feeling as if he's losing his mind.

As he once more enters the ICU, he now finds a soldier posted by Katie's door. Seeing Graham approach, the soldier rises to stop him, but then Dr. Jarvis arrives to usher Graham in.

Back by Katie's bedside, he listens as Jarvis explains that, as earlier, they cannot detect any physical injuries to her organs, much less anything else that could cause her degenerative symptoms:

This leaves, Mr. Lewis, physiological or emotional trauma.

As Graham stares at him, not knowing who or what to believe, Jarvis continues:

Time, unfortunately, is not on your wife's side.

Jarvis then leaves, leaving Graham staring down at Katie, his mind filling with ever more anguish and frustration.

Graham steps out of the hospital's entrance, reeling, lost, not knowing what to do or where to go.

But then an idea strikes him, a vague, perhaps inconclusive gambit, but it's all he has to go on, so he moves off, determined.

Just then a Taxicab happens to be by the hospital's entrance, and he quickly waves it down.

Climbing in, he gives the driver his address, but also instructions to drop him off a few blocks from home.

The Cabby nods without looking back and flips down the fare lever as he pulls away from the curb, heading back to the suburbs.

At first, Graham thinks nothing of the driver's silence.

But as the cab leaves the city center, traversing the steel bridge over the black river, Graham becomes suspicious.

He checks the cabbie's ID card on the taxi's dashboard to find an Arabic name, which the cabbie seems to notice and smiles as if he's used to it:

My father was a Muslim, my mother a Christian, but I was raised by a Jewish, Foster care family. So what does that make me?

Graham eases:

A potent combo?

A Holy war! And all fighting for the same God, I might add.

Graham smiles, appreciating the cabbie's welcome sense of humor.

What are you?

Graham shakes his head:

Me? Nothing.... No, I take that back. I'm a realist.

And what do realists, such as yourself, believe?

We believe in what's real.

The driver nods, still not looking back and then asks:

Define real?

Graham's about to launch into a practiced explanation, but then pauses, not so sure, and offers an argument even he's beginning to doubt:

Real's reality. What you can see, touch and feel.

The taxi suddenly swerves to the side of the road and pulls to a stop. Graham looks up, alarmed:

What are you doing?

We're here. A block away, as you requested.

Graham looks out to see they have indeed arrived.

Amazed at how quickly they made it, he climbs out and only then realizes he doesn't have any cash.

Listen, really sorry, but my wallet's at my house. So if you could just wait here a moment, I'll—

But the Taxi drives away, leaving Graham to watch after him, confused.

Minutes later, approaching his home, he sneaks over to the Honda, locates a hide-a-key attached under its rear wheel well, and, using it to gain entry, climbs in, fires it up and drives away, checking his rear view to see if he's being followed.

But instead of heading back to the city, he turns towards the mountains and the lab.

Climbing his way back up the mountain highway, he comes upon the now familiar bend in the road, the place where he and Leo first came upon the accident, and, finding no signs of an accident, quickly pulls over to the side.

He climbs out and inspects the pavement, searching for any signs of a crash – any debris fragments such as a glass piece, or a piece of broken tail light. Anything.

But he doesn't find a thing. Not even a skid mark.

Confounded yet again, Graham looks around, wondering if he's losing his mind in small, incremental stages.

He then climbs back into the Honda, makes a U-Turn and speeds back down the mountain.

As Graham marches back into the hospital's ICU, he finds a new soldier posted by Katie's door. As he approaches the soldier braces for action:

Don't come any closer, sir.

I'm her husband.

Sorry, sir, but only authorized hospital personnel are allowed in.

Graham pulls out his wallet and displays his driver's license:

Now, if you don't mind?

Soldier cocks his rifle:

I'm going to need you to clear this area, sir.

I'm not going anywhere, my friend.

The soldier trains his rifle:

Clear the area now!

What are you going to do, shoot me?

Soldier flips on his laser site, leveling its red dot on Graham's forehead:

I'm still not going anywhere, pal.

As the soldier braces, prepared to shoot, Emily runs up:

Stop it!

She moves between Graham and the soldier:

Like we need another patient in here? This is her husband!

My orders are to—

Protect her. But not from her husband!

The soldier eyes her, unsure now what to do.

Let him in . . . on my authority.

Soldier finally relents, and Graham and Emily quickly enter to find Katie fading, looking even more fragile, her breathing now driven by a respirator.

Where's Dr. Jarvis?

Emily looks around to make sure no one can hear her and then informs him:

I don't think Dr. Jarvis's your wife's friend.

Graham eyes her:

What are you saying?

Ever since he put himself in charge of her case, he's been prescribing all kinds of pills and crap, and all she's gotten is worse.

Graham stares, stunned as Emily continues:

If I was you, I'd get her the hell out of here before he kills her.

And take her where?

Anywhere! Just get her away from here.

But why would he...?

Wanna kill her? You tell me, but somebody's putting on a heck of a show for some damn reason.

Emily indicates the soldier by the door as being part of that show.

Graham considers it and starts to believe she may be right:

Would you help me?

As Emily sobers, apparently worried for her own safety, Jarvis sweeps into the room, obviously upset:

What's going on here?

Graham turns:

What do you mean?

I mean why are you here when your wife should be resting?

Jarvis shoots a reproving look at Emily:

And that includes you!

Graham's heard enough:

I've decided to check her out of this hospital.

Jarvis is shocked:

What?! No, you can't. And as her physician, I forbid it!

Look, I appreciate all you've done, but I'm her husband.

Now Graham moves to undo her IV's:

That I.V., which you are so eager to disconnect, may well be the only thing standing between her and a massive seizure.

Graham hesitates, glancing at Emily, who goes mum under Jarvis's attention. A moment later, Katie's EKG machine suddenly sounds its alarm.

Jarvis pushes Emily aside to watch its spiking, uneven readout...

Paddles!

Graham looks on horrified as Emily, scared to do otherwise, helps Jarvis prepare the defibrillator paddles.

Just as Jarvis's about to apply them, Katie's pulse normalizes, halting the alarm which abruptly shuts off.

Jarvis then sneers up at both Graham and Emily as if they were the cause:

I need you both to leave now. For her sake.

Graham nods, suddenly feeling dizzy. He tries to turn, but the world suddenly spins away from him and he collapses on to the floor.

An hour later, Jarvis finishes bandaging a fresh wound on Graham's cheek:

You have a concussion, Mr. Lewis. And you're just lucky you don't have a cracked skull to go with it.

Graham nods, accepting Jarvis's care now, grateful as Jarvis scribbles a prescription:

This will help with the headache. But I need you to stay off your feet for a while.

Thanks. And about earlier? Sorry if I...came on a little strong.

Jarvis seems to understand and shrugs:

If it was my wife, I don't know what I'd do.

Jarvis offers an understanding nod and departs.

Graham sits there a moment, trying to get his mental and emotional bearings. He takes a deep breath, trying to center himself, then pulls back on his shirt, slides off the table and heads out, determined to somehow extricate Katie.

But as he moves through the quiet emergency room, still adjusting his shirt, he suddenly slows and looks up to find the ward inexplicably empty.

He looks around to discover he's the only one there.

All the various medical stations and offices are vacant, abandoned.

Alarmed, he retraces his steps to see if he somehow took a wrong turn, but quickly realizes that this is the correct ward.

Doc ...Dr. Jarvis?

But only silence is the answer.

So he moves off, moving purposefully down the dimly-lit hallways, looking for a nurse, an orderly, anybody...

Finding no one, he heads for a bank of elevators and boards an open car, hitting third floor button, for Katie's floor.

Moments later, he steps off the elevator to find the third floor empty as well.

Beginning to panic, he moves on to the ICU to find its door ajar.

Rushing in, he finds Katie's room unguarded.

With his heart starting to pound into his throat, he enters Katie's room and finds it empty, too.

No, no, no!

Graham dodges back into the hallway, looks quickly around, and then runs for the stairwell...

Passing through the hospital's deserted lobby, he bursts back out onto the sidewalk to find it deserted, along with the hospital's parking lot across the street.

Even his Honda's gone.

Disconcerted, he starts to run, angling back towards the city, searching for any signs of life.

But as he moves along its sidewalks, he finds them dark and deserted as well – not a soul in sight anywhere, as if the whole world left for some other world, some other dimension.

As he starts searching ever more frantically, peering into darkened storefronts and banging on doors, he finally backs his way into the middle of a city street to shout up at the buildings:

Hello? Is anybody there?

But no one replies.

As he struggles to comprehend what is happening, he hears a low, guttural growl.

He turns, focusing on a pair of eyes glinting back at him from the shadows up the block.

As Graham strains to make them out, a snarl replaces the growl, and, as it paws its way into view under the flickering street light, he realizes he's looking into the blood-shot eyes of a large, black wolf.

Graham freezes, trying not to provoke it. He then starts backing ever-so-slowly away.

But the wolf snarls again, galvanizing itself for an attack as Graham steps back onto the sidewalk and eases back to a street corner.

As the wolf hunkers down its shoulders, preparing to lunge, Graham dodges out of the wolf's view around the street corner and dashes up the block.

But as he runs, he begins to feel like lead, just as the wolf starts clawing its way around the corner and then charging after him, quickly closing the gap.

Graham, straining to get his legs to work, turns another corner to see a Honda parked just up the street, looking very much like his own Honda.

So he angles incredulously for it as the wolf quickly makes up ground.

Arriving at the Honda, he fumbles for his keys and finally gets the door open and dives into the driver's seat, just as the wolf leaps at the door, slamming into it to claw at the Honda's window.

Graham finally manages to start the Honda and he accelerates away into the night, quickly outdistancing the wolf's attempts to keep pace.

Speeding through the dark, deserted city streets, his adrenaline pumping, he continues his search for any signs of life.

But it's useless. No one's here. And just as he begins to be certain he's alone, he makes one more turn, only to see the wolf again, bounding out of the shadows into the middle of the road.

Graham swerves, veering hard to the left, only to crash into a light pole, prying open the driver's side door.

As he struggles to restart the Honda, the wolf pounces again, squeezing its vicious teeth into the narrow opening of the door to snap at Graham, craving his flesh.

Graham, leaning as far left as he can, finally gets the Honda's motor to rev to life and throws it into gear. As it jerks forward, gaining speed, the wolf – half in, half out – digs its claws into the seat, determined to hang on as Graham swerves back and forth, trying to loosen its grip.

With one last hard turn to the right, he jettisons the wolf and accelerates away.

When he checks his rear view mirror, worried that the wolf is still giving chase, he's stunned to discover there's no sign of the wolf; just a shadowed, empty street in his back.

As Graham's mind scrambles, he veers onto the dark steel bridge, escaping the city and crossing the black river, but with no clue as to how, or where, to find Katie.

And then it hits him:

The lab.

A short time later, he screeches back into his driveway, jumps out and runs into his home.

Bounding up to the bedroom, he scrambles to find Katie's keycard again.

As he rifles through her drawer, he suddenly realizes that Cha-Cha is peering strangely into the bedroom, as if it senses a presence, but can't actually see Graham.

Hey, girl!

But Cha-Cha looks through him, sniffs the air, and then barks and quickly retreats as if she'd seen a ghost.

Graham stares after her:

Cha-Cha?

But with no time to lose, he relocates the keycard and the paper with 'Anniversary' scribbled on it and heads back out.

A moment later, he runs back out to the Honda, jumps in, and heads back for the mountains, this time for the lab.

Winding his way back up the highland highway, Graham rounds that now familiar bend to come upon the accident scene, suddenly flashing again with emergency vehicles.

Graham brakes in utter disbelief to view the horrific head-on collision, catching glimpses of an obscured victim receiving CPR as another is quickly loaded into an ambulance.

Somebody suddenly pounds the hood of the Honda, shocking Graham's attention to sufficiently realize that a Highway Patrolman is waving him on.

So Graham drives on, still eyeing the crash in his rear view mirror as he continues onto the lab.

Pulling into the facility's empty parking lot, he climbs out, looks quickly around and then heads for the entrance.

Using Katie's keycard, and the password 'anniversary', he gains access and makes his way through the series of security doors to the lab itself.

He finds it quiet as he steps in; he also finds the console lights actively blinking, running Mindfall.

As he moves to get a better view of the console, he suddenly sees the dark outlines of two bodies lying in the tech recliners.

Graham freezes and then realizes that the bodies aren't moving.

So Graham edges forward, straining to make out their features, advancing in the dark until he startles to realize: one of the bodies is Leo's, and the other is…his own.

Graham stops short; his mind momentarily becoming blank as he stares at himself, lying there unconscious in the dark.

Then, as if on some nightmarish cue, he hears the thundering pulse of a chopper descending again overhead.

Graham runs out of the lab to see on a closed-circuit image a SWAT team storming the facility's entrance again, while another fills onto its roof.

He hesitates, wondering if this time he should stay and face the soldiers, but then looks back at the lab, wondering what the SWAT will do with the unconscious bodies in the lab. But then what if that too is a trick, another convoluted turn of the program.

But as the footfalls of soldiers pound over the roof, he opts for escape, and heads again for that back exit.

Arriving at the Emergency Exit, he finds it locked. So he's forced to reverse pivot and run back in the direction of the oncoming SWAT team.

Seeing the approaching flicker of their laser sites flashing in the hallway, he slips into a side room, quickly locks its door and then hides in the dark, not knowing what else to do.

Moments later, a SWAT member tries the door, turning its handle until it stops.

Graham holds his breath, sure he's about to be discovered, but soon the door handle eases back into place and the sounds of footfalls move off again, heading down the hall.

Timing himself, Graham unlocks the door and cracks it open to look out; the SWAT team moving off in the direction of the lab.

So he slides from the room and hurries back up the hall, angling for the facility's entrance. As he nears it, he can see the thundering black chopper lower briefly into view, so he dives behind a reception desk as its rotors pump the air with a concussive force before lifting away again.

He peeks out from behind the reception desk; he can see the Honda where he parked it, but now obscured by two military Humvees.

So once again timing his move, he makes a run for it – out of the facility's entrance, and towards his Honda, as the chopper's blinding beam searches the tree-line.

Keeping low, Graham makes to his Honda, climbs in and starts it up – its motor drowned out by the chopper's pumping rotors – and eases back onto the highway, only to be discovered by the team on the roof.

So he throws into gear and steps down hard on the accelerator as bullets fly after him.

As the ground team rushes back to their Humvees, the chopper swoops and veers off after Graham as the Honda gains speed, racing back down the winding, mountain highway.

He fumbles for his cell phone and Joe's business card while simultaneously trying to drive, finally managing to dial Joe's number. As the call connects, he yells:

Hello... Hello?

But there's no response:

Hello?

In his rear view mirror, he can see the Humvees gaining on him as the connection seems to go dead, forcing him to have to dial it again as he swerves around corners, trying to outrun the Humvees.

And just as the call finally reconnects, he's rammed by a Humvee from behind, jettisoning the cell phone from his hand.

He accelerates again, trying to use the next bend in the road to gain some separation. But the Humvees accelerate too, quickly narrowing the gap until one rams him again.

The Honda fishtails, causing Graham to swerve out of control just as a pair of oncoming headlights whip around the turn ahead, instantly bearing down on him, its headlights scorching his vision, blinding him as he barrels into them, into the crushing impact, only to suddenly bolt up to find himself back in the lab.

He looks around, breathing hard, terrified but alive, and suddenly alone again in the dark, silent room.

He looks to the chair next to him to find it empty. No sign of Leo.

He then listens, but can't hear sounds or sings of any SWAT team assault.

He climbs from the chair and moves to the lab's door.

Cracking it cautiously open, he views the hallway, quiet and undisturbed.

So he starts for it, noting the peaceful views of the facility's exterior on the security camera views.

As he steps out of its entrance, his eyes squint to see the dawn breaking over the mountain top as the facility's sprinklers draw lazy circles on its lawn. Some songbirds chirp cheerfully in the nearby trees, greeting the new day.

In the parking lot, he finds Leo's Toyota truck, right where he parked on that first visit, and yet there's no sign of his Honda.

So he moves cautiously to it, finds its keys on its seat, climbs in, and, not knowing what else to do, drives slowly out of the facility.

As he travels back down the highway, he comes upon the bend in the road, but sees no sign of the accidents.

Later, as he drives through his neighborhood, he sees his neighbors mowing their lawns, or watching their children play. One waves to him, so he waves back.

As Graham steps into his home, reeling, expecting to find it empty, he hears:

Honey? That you?

Graham nearly falls on hearing Katie's gentle voice.

Too stunned to move, he stands there, shaking as she comes in from the back yard to find him, smiling as she dusts off some potting soil from her hands.

When she sees him standing there, all but trembling, she smiles:

What' is it, honey?

Graham stares at her, unable to formulate the words.

You all right? You look like you've seen a ghost.

As his eyes boil up with tears, she moves to him, newly concerned:

Hey, you okay?

As she folds her arms around him, he latches onto her as if to never let her go again.

Is something wrong? Did something happen?

All Graham can manage is to shake his head as Cha-Cha bounds up giddily:

You sure?

Graham pulls back to look at Katie, wanting desperately to believe this is real, but not sure if he can...

She eyes him softly and then pulls him to her again. He sinks into her embrace, still overcome to speak:

Think I'll have to do more gardening!

He finally manages to dribble out:

...You have no idea.

She eyes him:

What is it, honey?

I'm just so...happy you're here. That you're okay.

Well of course I'm okay, love! You're the weirdo in this family.

Graham laughs and buries his face in her neck:

46

…You have no idea.

He then pulls back that so he can tell her:

When I woke up I couldn't find you, so I went to the lab, but you weren't there.

She shrugs:

We must've just missed each other.

He eyes her, unable to explain more, but also because he does not want to.

Later that day, Graham is playing dodge-the-hose-water with Cha-Cha, who playfully fakes left, then right, then left again as Graham adjusts his aim.

Katie is meanwhile on her knees in a flower bed, planting a new row of calalilies:

I still can't believe he took you to the lab. He should never have done that. It only puts you under suspicion. I'm going to have to speak to Leo about that.

Not today, okay?

She looks up, noting his adamant tone:

Let's just have this day for us, okay? Just one day. Whatever day this is!

She climbs to her feet and hugs him:

I don't know what happened to you, but I gotta say: I kinda like it.

Just then, their house phone rings. As Katie moves off to answer it, he calls after her:

If it's Leo—

I'll let the machine get it!

As Katie goes back into the house, Cha-Cha suddenly starts running exuberant laps around the back yard. Graham laughs at her antics, finally beginning to ease:

I feel ya, Cha-Cha…Trust me, I feel ya.

As the gentle day fades quietly into afternoon, Graham lingers in his back yard, feeling the warm sun on his back and a Zephyr breeze on his skin.

Daydreaming, he watches a darting squirrel go about his earnest business and then takes in a blue butterfly's delicate dance in and out of some white and yellow orange blossoms.

Katie sees him daydreaming and comes out, soothed, to see his peace. They share a loving, knowing smile.

It's really beautiful out here.

Katie smiles.

It is. So, you okay?

Graham considers, shrugs, unable to make any sense of:

Think I was in Mindfall.

Something in Katie's gaze sobers, deepens.

And I gotta say it was terrible. Like a nightmare on an endless loop.

Katie is listening carefully as Graham continues:

And everything else seemed – seems – almost unreal by comparison.

She eyes him:

The thing is, honey, you just have to try to let it go. And I mean all of it. Even your ideas about it. About everything, really. Because as long as you keep holding onto them like they're real, you can't...move on with your life.

Not sure what she means, he draws in a deep breath:

All I know is right now it's just so nice to stand here, with nowhere to go and nothing to do.

She smiles understandingly and rubs his back.

Let go of it, darling because until you do, it won't let go of you.

He looks at her, not sure what she's referring to:

Let go of what?

All the head stuff that gets in the way of just, as you say, being here.

As he stares at her, sensing she wants him to understand something he doesn't yet, she smiles:

I better start getting ready.

For what?

Bill and Julie are coming over for dinner.

Later, as Graham selects something to wear, he comes across his shirt with the red wine stain.

He eyes it a moment and then shrugs, trying to let it go, still unable to fit any of the pieces together. All he knows is how good it is to have it all behind him.

As seven o'clock rolls around, their doorbell dings, and Katie, looking radiantly beautiful in a diaphanous dress, opens their door to greet Bill and Julie, who enter, already talking a blue streak as they hand off gifts of wine and flowers:

Hey, honey. Bill and Julie are here!

A jovial dinner conversation, spiced by Bill and Julie's running repartee, suddenly veers towards the philosophic, offering Bill a segue-way into one of his old saw-horse topics:

Okay I have a question for you: how do you define 'reality'?

Graham looks up, remembering the Cabbie's question as Julie groans. But Bill good-naturedly ignores her and looks to Graham, who responds innocently:

You asking me?

No, I'm lecturing you, actually, but go with me.

Julie guffaws:

'Lecturing' is right!

Undismayed, Bill presses on:

I mean here we are, seated around this lovely table, surrounded by all these 'real' things, yes? Katie's always magnificent pasta Bolognese, antipasto and a most excellent, coquettish Cabernet, if I do say so myself.

Katie grins:

Thank you for the wine, Bill.

But Bill's already moving on:

They look and feel real.

Julie chimes in:

And taste amazingly real.

Bill presses on:

And seem in all ways actual and solid, and yet even the most basic study of Physics reveals that all solids – all this 'real' stuff – is, at its most basic, fundamental level, light. Just light!

He clearly loves this part of his lecture:

So if we try to define real as being things that are solid, when all solids are actually non-solid light energy, then what do we mean by 'real' – because as far as I'm concerned, when anybody says 'real', they mean only what they can see.

Katie volunteers:

Or believe.

Exactly!

Graham grins:

Nice one, honey.

My point, or the fact that I got a word in edge-wise?

That you got a word in edge-wise.

But Bill isn't done:

Because what they can see – or believe – is based entirely and only on what they're able to comprehend, where as time...

Julie looks heavenward for help:

Please tell me this won't take much more time.

But Bill continues, not bothered:

Time, which we think of as an unchangeable constant, turns out to, as any astrophysicist will tell you, actually speed up or slow down depending on where you are in the universe. Heck, there may be places where it even stops!

Julie can't resist:

Unlike this lecture, interestingly enough.

Bill looks past her, appealing to Graham and Katie:

Do you see what genius has to endure in this world?

Katie grins:

All I know is if I ever find the place or planet where time stops, I'm moving there yesterday!

A woman's prerogative. My point, before anybody else rudely interrupts me, is that if so-called solid objects aren't solid, and time isn't constant, reality is, was, and never will be what we think, but something impermanent and changing and ultimately as elastic as any other theory of reality. And there, boys and girls, my lecture ends.

Bill looks to Graham, expecting him to weigh in:

Well, Graham, have you lost all your piss and vinegar when it comes to my poetic ramblings on the nature of existence?

Graham grins, taking up the challenge:

If ya ask me...

They all wait –

I think you're full of crap.

Bill lets out a blast of laughter:

That's my man! I was starting to worry about you. Only thing worse would have been if I started to make the case for life after death!

Katie raises a toast:

To the here and now, and to all that we don't know or understand about life, and to life itself . . .

She then adds, especially for Graham:

Even if it's a life after death, beyond anything our minds can conceive.

Graham smiles wryly, and raises his glass:

Cheers.

Later that night, in bed, Graham spoons up to Katie:

You're my life.

Katie turns to kiss him and then rolls back to fall asleep in his arms. But as she does, her gaze fills with knowing – somber, unexpressed concern for Graham's journey, yet to come.

Later, a faintly ticking clock keeps vigil as Graham sleeps, quietly marking the seconds, only to abruptly stop.

A silence falls.

Graham stirs in the dark as if awakened by its absence.

He gropes for the bed-stand lamp, still sleepy.

Flipping on a pale light, he rolls over to find a scribbled note in Katie's place.

Still groggy, he takes it up to read:

'See you soon, my love'.

Graham rolls over to sleep…but then suddenly rears back up in horror.

Katie?

He bolts out of bed to check in their bathroom:

Katie?

A knock thunders up from the front door, shattering the silence.

Graham whips around, feeling the undertow of the nightmare again as another knock demands his response.

Then another knock, louder and more insistent, rattles through the house, and Cha-Cha, resting nearby, jumps up to bark at it.

He calls to her:

It's okay, girl.

Gathering himself, he moves downstairs to answer it.

Stepping up to his front door's peephole, he fearfully peers out to see agent Saunders, just as before, flanked by the junior agents.

Mr. Lewis?

What do you want?

It's concerning your wife, Mr. Lewis.

Moments later, Graham finds himself being rushed once more from his house into the black van, and then on to the shadowed city.

He peers out the van's window as the dark world races past, seeing a ghostly image of himself suspended in the glass reflection.

Looking beyond the reflection, he can see the dark, steel bridge coming into view.

Mr. Lewis?

Graham turns to agent Saunders:

We'll be there shortly, sir.

Graham eyes him a moment, noting this small, new wrinkle in this recapitulating drama, and then looks back out as the van rumbles over the bridge.

Below, the black river waters glimmer under a pale moon as Graham's mind turns, teetering on its own edge.

Graham walks into the hospital's now-busy lobby, flanked by the agents, expecting to be greeted by Dr. Jarvis.

Instead, he catches a glimpse of Emily, who seems to dodge away as if trying to avoid him.

As he watches after her, confused, Jarvis does indeed arrive, extending his hand as if for the first time:

Mr. Lewis? I'm Dr. Jarvis.

But Graham is already on his way to the Intensive Care Unit:

Mr. Lewis?

Graham hurries to Katie's bedside to find her unconscious, just as before, but this time already breathing through a ventilator.

As he eyes her incredulously with deep anguish, he hears:

Graham?

Graham whips around to find Br. Ananda. He stares at him in disbelief:

What are you...?

Ananda looks confused:

I only just got your voice mail.

Voice mail?

About Katie.

From who?

You!

As Graham remembers the message he left that first night, Ananda continues:

I also got a text from Leo.

Where is he?

Leo? I don't know. I thought I might find him here with you.

Graham's mind can't help but seize on the irony:

'Here'? So just where is here?

Ananda is not sure what Graham means, but he indicates he'd like to move closer to Katie's bedside:

May I?

Graham nods, and Ananda moves forward to take her hand, uttering a quiet prayer for her care and protection and then looks back to Graham:

Is there anything I can do?

Graham looks at Ananda fixedly:

Explain it. Can you do that?

Ananda reflects quietly and then murmurs:

...No. But I can stay here with you, if that's all right.

Mr. Lewis?

Graham turns again to see Joe, flanked by two soldiers, standing outside Katie's room:

We need to talk.

At the sight of Joe, a growing anger begins to replace Graham's confusion:

Not now.

But Joe insists:

I'm sorry, but it really does need to be now.

Ananda tries to reassure Graham:

You go. I'll stay here.

Joe and two soldiers escort a reluctant Graham down several hallways to a closed-off area.

Joe then motions for the soldiers to guard their privacy as he guides Graham out of their earshot while Graham grows increasingly impatient:

What do you want?

Last night we intercepted several communiqués from The Burning Sky, indicating they're planning a major attack. In short, as we speak, all roads in and out the city are being closed, and a door-to-door search for Ahn Li and his associates is already underway.

And Army Captain enters the ward, spots Joe and angles towards him:

Sir?

Joe looks up:

A strike force is now in place at the power plant.

How about the water-treatment facility?

Any moment now, sir.

Not good enough, Captain. They should already be in position!

Yes, sir!

As the Captain hustles out, Joe turns back to Graham:

On the other hand, Ahn Li and the Burning Sky may just be using the threat of an attack to divert our attention, spread our resources, all in an effort to gain access to Katie.

Graham stares at Joe as if he's just part of a dream world.

Thrown by Graham's strange expression, Joe cocks his head:

Do you understand what I'm saying to you, Mr. Lewis? We are in a race against time now, which is why I've made arrangements for you and Katie to be moved to a secure location outside of the city. Do you understand what I'm saying to you?

Graham ponders it and then calmly responds:

You're not taking Katie anywhere.

Joe is startled, taken by surprise:

I'm afraid, Mr. Lewis, that is not your decision.

Not my decision? She's my wife!

Joe sobers:

Under the circumstances, Mr. Lewis, your marriage vows are the very least of my concerns.

Who gave you the authority?

Joe looks amused by the question:

Isn't it obvious?

No.

Joe gets up and adjusts his jacket:

I am the Sysmin of this system, Mr. Lewis. Or hadn't you figured that out yet?

Graham balks:

Sysmin of what?

Joe smiles:

Why, this system, of course, Mr. Lewis.

'This system'?

Joe looks surprised by Graham's confusion:

We are all subject to a system, yes? A world. A reality. A state of awareness. Your state of awareness, Mr. Lewis. And that is what makes you subject to this system, thereby giving me the authority over you, or rather, your state of awareness, which is to say, your reality.

As Graham recoils, sensing a terrible truth wending its way to his awareness, they hear the sudden thunder of approaching footfalls, drawing their attention to a contingent of heavily-armed soldiers as they hustle in:

What is it?

A Sergeant steps forward:

She's gone, sir.

Who's gone?

The Sergeant tries to indicate Graham, not wanting to mention Katie by name, but it doesn't matter. They all know who he means. Joe is enraged:

What do you mean she's 'gone'?

She's not in her room, sir.

So find her!

As they hustle back out, Joe casts a look back at Graham:

Good day, Mr. Lewis.

Joe leaves, nodding something to the two soldiers as he departs.

When Graham tries to follow him, the soldiers instantly close ranks behind him, assigned to guard him, yes, but also restrict what he can do.

As they escort him back up the hallway, their presence all but denying him his freedom, Graham begins looking for a way to ditch them.

Looking ahead, he sees a familiar bank of elevators and then the custodian mopping the floor, and an elevator car door opens to deliver the hospital orderly, who starts backing out pulling a tall, teetering food cart, filled with meal trays out onto the floor. Graham's eyes burn with recognition, waking up to the recapitulating scene from before as it unfolds once more before his eyes.

This time, just as the orderly trips once more over the custodian's mop, grabbing onto the food cart to break his fall, causing the cart to topple over and crash it to the floor, Graham whips around to catch the momentarily distracted soldiers off-guard.

He punches the closest one, knocking him down, and then tackles the second into the wall, where Graham is able to strip his gun.

As the first soldier grabs for his side-arm, Graham throws the second soldier onto him and takes off down the hall, dodging not only the fallen food trays, but also two errant shots from the soldiers.

Graham dodges down a connecting hallway, out of their view as the soldiers scramble back to their feet.

Graham, running, spots a stairwell and bangs into it.

Moments later, the soldiers race past, missing Graham's trick as Graham hustles down three floors to the lobby.

Graham eases out of the lobby's stairwell door to deftly navigate the now busy hospital reception area.

But as he angles towards the entrance, he sees more soldiers standing guard outside, checking all who wish to enter or leave.

So Graham doubles back and moves out of their view and then looks around in need of a diversion, and spots a humble but effective fire alarm perched on a wall.

Moving to it casually, he suddenly breaks its protective glass and flips its lever, triggering a sudden downpour.

As the lobby quickly devolves into a rainy chaos, with patients and their families charging for the exits, Graham slips into their drenched ranks and pushes forward with them, lost in their numbers as they force themselves out onto the sidewalk, overwhelming the soldiers' ability to keep control.

Graham then slips away unnoticed and hurries off into the dark as a crack of thunder seems to trigger another downpour, drenching the city in a sudden deluge.

On the move, Graham keeps checking behind him, sure that the soldiers will soon be on his heels.

Turning down a dark block, he's forced to dodge into the shadows of a doorway as a Humvee full of soldiers races up the block, brakes hard and deposits two soldiers, who hustle down the street as the Humvee speeds off again into the rain.

Relieved, he slumps, drawing in a deep breath, taking this moment to rest and recoup, to somehow gather up all that's happened and come up with a plan, only to hear:

Don't move!

Graham freezes, thinking it's one of the soldiers.

But a moment later, a desperate street thug moves into view, training a desperate gun at him, trying to look fearsome, but clearly scared. Graham endures this mugging as if from a surreal distance, seeing it all, more and more, as unreal.

But to the thug, this clearly means everything:

Give me your watch, dude, and I mean now!

Graham hands it over, feeling a certain compassion for the thug's fraught attempt to feel powerful.

Now your wallet.

Graham obeys and hands it over. The thug rifles through it, angered to find it empty, and throws it away.

You better have somethin' on ya, or I'm gonna goddamn blow you away, dude!

I'd give you my life, but it's not my own anymore, and trust me, you wouldn't want it.

The thug, confused but very angry, considers shooting Graham, but then uses the butt of his gun to strike Graham across the back of the back and runs.

Graham, out on his feet, crumples forward unconscious, into the fast-moving rush of runoff rain water swelling the gutter. As he lies there, in danger of drowning as the water rises, submerging him, the sound of gushing water changes; the 'shhh' transforms into the sound of running faucet-water, circling into a wash sink.

Graham's eyes slowly open to see tap-water swirling the drain in one direction, then slowing and reversing its direction, and then slowing and reversing course once more.

He then watches as his hands cup some faucet water and bring it up to splash onto his face.

Straightening up, he finds a mirror over the sink, and sees the young boy he was looking curiously back at him, at the age of six.

Graham leans over the sink again, cupping more water and splashing it over his face. Now he straightens back up to see himself as an old man, only to watch the image fade as the rush of running faucet water fades into the din of a party.

As the mirror goes dark, he realizes he's standing in his own home's guest bathroom, once more hearing the lively chatter and music of his anniversary party.

Graham slumps, his mind reeling, his emotions spinning.

He looks back at himself in the mirror, trying to hold onto what's left of his sanity, his sense of self, his sense of…anything.

Re-gathering himself, he cracks the bathroom door open to see the party underway, just as before.

As he watches, seeing Bill, then Julie, and then Katie, his eyes fill with tears, but he closes the door again, unable to continue; surely it's all just some kind of nightmare or hologram meant to torture him.

But then a knock on the door compels a response.

Graham? Graham? I know you're in there.

Recognizing Julie's voice, he finally relents and opens the door.

Told ya you were in there! Now if you don't mind…

She pulls him out so that she can use the bathroom.

As he stands outside the bathroom's door, he watches the others, not wanting to engage them and thus reengage the loop in his nightmare.

But he also knows he can't go backwards. Mindfall apparently won't permit it.

So he stands there, unable to move forward or backwards, observing the party as if from a great distance, or from another dimension, seeing their joy, their friendship, and the world he knew, but didn't quite allow himself to wholly feel, to never quite fully embrace, to never fully engage alive before him.

Compelled by this vision, he moves through the room as if through a menagerie, observing his friends' faces, hearing their laughter, feeling the music, yet haunted by the knowledge that it's all just an illusion, a trick.

His gaze suddenly sharpens, darkens as he suddenly looks around, searching the room for anyone else who just might see what he's seeing, whose expression could reveal that they see what he sees.

Instead, he sees Katie introducing Br. Ananda to the couple, just as before.

So he moves towards them, angling into earshot:

And Brother Ananda married us.

I was only doing my job.

Ananda then looks over at Graham as if expecting his response. But Graham resists, refusing to play along.

There you are!

Katie is beaming, smiling as she turns to hug and kiss him:

Thought we'd lost you!

There he is!

Graham turns again to see Bill approaching, and Graham searches his eyes for any flicker of recognition. But Bill just smiles and joins in with Katie's hug:

What a great party!

Graham, unable to smile, looks down:

You okay, honey?

Bill, sensing something's wrong, nods to Katie and retreats, offering them their momentary privacy as Graham looks back up to search her eyes:

This isn't...

What, honey? This isn't what?

Katie's face fills with concern as Graham struggles to say what's clearly crushing him.

A moment later, Graham feels himself backing away from her, trying to extricate himself emotionally, worried that he night reinvest in this illusion, this dimension, only to have it dashed, too, like the last one.

As Katie watches after him, now deeply concerned, Graham navigates his way to the patio door, lost in his own hell as various guests pat his back.

Stepping out into the night, he takes a moment to catch his breath, feeling like a man who's just survived drowning. He then recalls the last time this happened, and looks around for Leo. But he's not here.

So Graham moves over to self-serve bar to find what looks like Leo's abandoned drink. He looks once more around to no avail, then refocuses on the bar before him, and takes a bottle of Cabernet wine.

Pouring himself a glass, he takes a gulp, winces at the taste and spits it out. As he wipes his mouth, he hears:

Hey, Graham, how about a toast?

Graham turns to see Bill, flanked by several other guests on the patio, raising their glasses in his honor:

Graham eyes their expectant faces, and knows they are ready for Graham to say something sweet and moving.

But what follows is a long, awkward silence as Graham stares at them as if they were all shadows.

As the guests look around at each other with surprise and a growing concern, sensing something's very wrong. Then Graham tosses out:

Does it matter what I say? What anyone of us says, or thinks, or believes, for that matter?

Katie, stepping out onto the patio, moves in front of Bill, her face full of compassion and fear:

Honey, is something wrong?

Graham scrutinizes her carefully and then scrutinizes the others as well – surely all this is just one more emulation reality field, one bend in Mindfall's endless loop:

I get it.
Get 'what'?
That we're all not really here. That this is all just...
Just what?
One more turn of the kaleidoscope.

Katie's coming to the point of tears:

What are you, love?
I'm talking about this.

Graham gestures, indicating the party, the night, the world:

Whatever 'this' is.

Bill steps forward again, concerned:

Hey, brother, what's up?

Graham looks to Bill, beginning to see all this now as a prison:

You don't know? None of you know? So what are you, holograms? Cognitive emulations with no minds of your own?

Everyone's now staring at Graham. The music has stopped, and the party's come to an abrupt, shocked halt.

You're all looking at me as if I'm crazy. But I'm not crazy, and this has to stop.

He turns back to Katie:

Make it stop, Katie. Make this thing you created...

But he catches himself.

But you're not Katie, are you?
What?

Because if you were, and if all this was real, where's Leo, huh? He should be here. But he isn't, is he?

When they all just stare back at him, Graham grabs the Cabernet bottle and heaves it through the large, living room window, that looks out on the patio, shattering it.

Bill steps forward:

Jesus, Graham! What the hell's going on?

Graham shrugs, balking, filled with the black irony of it all:

With me? Nothing. I'm just screwed. Just like you're screwed. Just like we're all screwed!

As the gusts trade horrified looks, Bill tries to talk Graham down:

So we're all screwed. I hear ya, bro. So let's talk about that.

Great, we'll do lunch!

Look, everything's going to be cool, my man, so let's just all settle down, okay? We good?

Graham balks:

Will it be cool? Really? Because far as I can tell, we're all just lost in this big loop, going around and around and around.

Bill's doing his best to reason with him:

I hear ya. But can we just talk about it? Talk about what's on your mind?

See, that's just it. I can't, cause 'on my mind' is the only place this even exists.

As Graham considers it, he starts to laugh. Bill's confused:

What?

It just dawned on me: not only is all of this an emulation, I am, too! A figment of my own imagination. Can ya beat that? Which is what: a figment of itself? That's the conundrum, isn't it? So who's imagining me? Who's the dreamer, and what's the dream? And why, why can't I wake up from it?

Bill and the others, having traded some subtle looks, are edging into a circle around Graham, slowly positioning themselves to rush him, which he quickly recognizes:

Careful, fellas. Or I might have to kick some serious realty emulation field ass!

He then suddenly sees Leo, in a corner of the yard, invisible to the others, just as he seems unconcerned by the others, raising a toast from the shadows:

Care to join me? It's a smooth ride to who knows where.

Graham, still keeping an eye on the encroaching guests, calls to him:

You know, don't you?

Leo grins coyly:

Know what?

We're still in Mindfall, are we?

Leo has to chuckle:

Yeah, well, whadaya gonna do?

So what are you doing here?

Leo shrugs:

Was gonna ask you the same thing.

Graham, seeing his friends moving into range, throws the mini-bar over on its side:

Back off!

Leo, unconcerned, continues:

But if this is all just your mind, what is it you're really trying to escape from?

Graham, trying to keep an eye on his friends, wants to hear Leo's answer. Leo smiles, and quotes Ananda:

'Are we these bodies? These thoughts? These little egos? Or are we rather like waves on an ocean?'

As Graham sobers, affected by Ananda's words, Bill feels that Graham is distracted and charges him, tackling him to the ground as others join in.

Graham struggles against them with all his strength, trying to wriggle out from under, when he is suddenly shocked awake in his bed, breathing hard…

His bedroom is dark and quiet, except for the solitary ticking of a small clock.

Reeling, he flips on the light and looks around to discover: he's in his bedroom again; Katie's gone, but there's the familiar scribbled note.

As Graham eyes it, agent Saunders' expected knock echoes up from below.

Moments later, Saunders and the other agents have to step aside as Graham marches out, ignoring Saunders' attempt to explain, and heads right for the van.

Saunders and his fellow agents look at each other, confused, and then hurry along to catch up with Graham.

As the team climb into the van, Graham suddenly reaches forward and grabs one of the agent's guns, and instantly trains it on Saunders:

Keys!

Saunders, taken off guard, assesses the situation and then nods to the driver agent, who hands over the keys:

Now get out. All of you.

The agents obey, and Graham quickly slides into the driver's seat and fires up the van, his weapon still trained on Saunders, who steps out last, and Graham instantly screeches out of his driveway, accelerating away into the night.

As Saunders calls for backup in his rear view mirror, Graham speeds through his neighborhood, eerily dark and quiet under a pale moon.

He then peels out onto the highway, angling towards the jagged skyline of the shadowed city looming in the distance.

But then he sees a line of flashing emergency lights in the distance, extending across the highway.

He slows, peering ahead, sensing trouble, and soon realizes it's a blockade, complete with a soldiers, an armored troop carrier and two Humvees.

Graham blanches and veers onto an exit, banging his fist on the steering well:

Goddamnit, goddamnit, goddamnit!

Now he's racing through a vaguely familiar neighborhood.

He glances around, feeling as though he knows this area, but not sure why until he sees a Church, and brakes hard.

He jumps out to get a better look, confirming his memory, then hops back in and swings into its parking lot, taking care to be out of view from the street.

He then hurries to a back door entrance, lit by a solitary light bulb, and knocks on the door, waits, and then knocks once again more firmly.

Still nothing.

So he heads around to another entrance and tries the door latch. To his surprise, it clicks open, and he enters the door interior.

Making his way forward, he sees the flicker of candlelight and realizes he is in the Church itself.

As he moves into the sanctuary from the side, coming upon its dark, serene altar under high-domed ceilings, he looks around, starting to remember his wedding day – the altar step on which he and Katie stood as Ananda led them though their vows, the smiling, loving faces of their friends and family glowing up from the now-empty pews, and the thoughts of a life together that filled him, giving him a peace he'd never before known.

He moves to the front pew and sinks into it, his eyes filling with tears and frustration and confusion. And as he sits there, leaning forward, his face falling into his hands, he hears:

Graham?

Graham, alarmed, rears around to see Ananda in his pajamas and holding a flashlight, coming down the aisle:

Is that you?

Graham's eyes are boring into Ananda, burning with pain and desperation as Ananda draws near:

What is it, Graham?

It's not real, is it? Any of it.

Ananda slows, sobering, his demeanor changing from that of a comforter, to that of a truth-teller:

...Come with me.

They enter the rectory to find a modestly furnished room with a small fireplace.

Ananda gestures and Graham takes a seat by the fireplace, where Ananda lights a small fire and then sits in an adjoining chair as the flames crackle to life.

Graham looks again to Ananda, still awaiting an answer as Ananda reflects:

Is it real? That depends on what you mean by 'real'.

Is Katie dead?

...No.

Then where is she? Where'd they take her?

...To the hospital's morgue.

Graham searches Ananda's eyes:

So she...died?

Ananda takes a moment to ponder it and then says:

Would you like to know the secret of death?

Graham winces incredulously.

The secret of death is that there is no death.

Graham's incredulity is quickly turning into rage.

Life goes on, Graham. So does Katie's. So does yours. All that holds us back from experiencing it is ourselves. Our own beliefs.

But Graham's seething about something Ananda said before, and he leaps up, livid.

She dies, they take her body to the morgue, and you didn't think to tell me?

But she's not dead.

Yes, she is! And you don't even have the human decency to admit it, even now!

But she's alive, Graham.

Bullshit! That's just the crap people pay you to say at funerals. So not only is none of this real, but neither are you. And the worst part is, you know it!

As Graham starts for the door, Ananda adds:

When I was in kindergarten, I thought I had the whole world figured out.

Graham turns, full of contempt:

But even by first grade, I realized there was more to the world than I had surmised in kindergarten, and so I had better expand my view. By second grade, I felt the same way about first grade. And so on and so forth, right to this very moment. My point is, just because you think you know the truth doesn't mean that thought is real, or will be true tomorrow.

Graham sneers, filled with even more disdain:

Great. An explanation without an answer! Placebos for a world in pain!

What is it that you really want to know, Graham?

Now?! Now all I want to know is how Mindfall works so that I can get the hell out of it!

Ananda eyes him, confused:

'Mindfall'?

Yes! Or are you going to try to mislead me about that, too?

Mindfall's just a mirror.

Ananda's phone rings. Surprised by the late call, Ananda answers it:

Hello ...It's for you.

Graham pales:

Says his name is Joe.

How did he...?

They suddenly hear the rumble of military personnel carriers rolling up outside.

Graham rushes to a window and peers out to see soldiers quickly disembarking to surround the Rectory.

Graham dodges back from the window:

You called them, you sonofabitch!

Graham starts checking various windows, searching for a way out. He then smashes a stained glass window, climbs out and drops down, nimbly avoiding detection behind the bushes alongside the Rectory.

Almost safe, he makes his way by a hedge, staying low, until the hedge ends.

Looking ahead, he sees another set of bushes he can use for cover, but he'll need to make a daring run across open space.

So, gathering himself, as laser gun-sights flicker in the night, he takes a deep breath and makes a run for it, only to suddenly trip and fly through the air...landing hard in a tumble. But before he can recover, the two SWAT men are on him, their rifles cocked:

Freeze!

Graham, his eyes burning, glares up at them:

If you're going to shoot, shoot!

One of the soldiers tips back his helmet to furtively reveal himself to be Seal:

Would ya shut your yap, mate?

The other soldier tips back his helmet, revealing it to be Roan. They then grab Graham under the armpits and whisk him into one of the SWAT Humvees, which they then fire up and speed away from the Church...

As they speed back towards the city, Graham looks at them:

What do you want?

Seal turns:

Your wife's still alive, brother. But not for much longer if you don't help us!

Graham grabs him:

You're sure?

Roan leans over:

Dude, we know it for a fact.

Graham responds feebly:

I'll do anything. Anything you want!

Crossing into the city, they pull inside an empty garage where an ambulance is waiting. Seal and Roan peel back their military fatigues to reveal ambulance attendant uniforms as they all climb into the ambulance.

When ya get to the morgue, mate, I want you to look for a bright green body bag marked 'infectious disease'. That'll be her.

Graham is shocked:

Hey, how many guys are gonna wanna open a body-bag marked like that?

Minutes later, amidst sirens blaring, they arrive again at the E.R. entrance to see armed guards manning the exits.

Seal and Roan jump out and run around to the back of the ambulance where the guards raise their rifles, at which Seal snarls:

He's one of yours, ya stupid bastards. Now give me a hand!

As Seal yanks open the ambulance's bay doors, the soldiers check with each other, not sure how to handle this:

Ya want him to die out here, do ya?

One of the soldiers steps forward and pulls back the sheet to find Graham, in army fatigues, covered in blood:

They instantly think better and move to lend Seal and Roan a hand. And together, they charge Graham's stretcher into the Emergency Room's waiting doors.

As Seal and Roan rush Graham deeper into the E.R., the soldiers peel off to return back to their posts.

Seal and Roan then wheel Graham into an empty emergency bay and yank its curtains closed.

Once out of view, Graham immediately sits up to strip off the bloody layer of army fatigues, as Seal keeps watch.

Graham then pulls on a physician's white coat, hidden under the stretcher's cushion, along with a stethoscope which he hangs around his neck.

Suddenly he's a doctor.

Seal and Roan nod 'good luck' and slip away as Graham pulls back the curtain and starts down the hall in the opposite direction, moving with the authority of a confident physician.

He exchanges collegial nods with the other doctors he passes, even as they register their unfamiliarity with him.

Amazed by his luck, Graham moves on past several SWAT team soldiers, who pass him by without so much as a second look.

But as he turns another corner, he comes upon the nurse from the ICU.

She instantly recognizes him, and quickly frowns with suspicion at his physician's garb:

Mr. Lewis? What are you...?

Graham presses on, making a beeline for an elevator down the hallway as the staff nurse calls after him and then hurries off to find a soldier.

Boarding the elevator, he presses the basement button and then bangs on it with his fist, trying to speed it up.

Its doors finally close, and the car begins its slow descent, sinking reluctantly as if into a dark underworld.

Graham finally steps out into the huge, dimly-lit catacombs of the basement.

When he enters the morgue, his breath instantly fogs the chilled air as he pushes aside two empty stretchers seen in an open autopsy room, with cadavers laid out on stainless steel beds in various states of decay.

He presses on to another large door, and enters it to find a warehouse-like storage facility – cavernous, with seemingly endless rows of stacked corpses covered by semi-clear plastic body bags, as far as the eye can see in the dim light.

Jesus...

He moves further into the immense repository, incredulous, overwhelmed, looking for any green-tagged corpses, only to discover aisles and aisles of green-tagged corpses.

Shaken and daunted by its incomprehensible size, Graham looks around, not even sure where or how to begin his search.

So he moves to the closest row of shelves and unzips the nearest green body bag to reveal a decaying corpse's face.

Graham gags back and then steadies himself enough to zip it back up so that he can move on to the next green bag.

Then another, and another, and another.

One after the other he unzips and zips the green bag, until he suddenly hears the morgue's steel door crank open.

His eyes dart, looking for somewhere to hide.

Spotting an empty space on one of the shelves further down, he hurries to it and hoists himself into one empty shelf space – just as a flash light beam glares into the corridor, panning from side to side.

As Graham holds his breath, the flash light beam starts moving down the corridor, approaching his hiding place.

So he tries to tilt his head to see who's wielding the light. As he does, the green body bag across the corridor seems to move, to shift slightly, instantly drawing Graham's attention as a voice suddenly says:

What are you doing here, Mr. Lewis?

Graham freezes again as the voice's owner continues to advance on Graham's hiding place, panning the flashlight from side to side.

I know you're here, Mr. Lewis. And you should know I've already contacted the authorities. They're on their way here now, so I suggest you best just give yourself up.

As Graham tries to sink further into the compartment to avoid detection, a flashlight beam pans over the green bag across from Graham; alerted to the presence of life there, the possessor of the light moves in to investigate, revealing himself to be Dr. Jarvis.

Jarvis, zeroing in like a hunting dog, unzips the bag to disclose Katie's woozy face.

But just as Jarvis' face flashes with recognition, he's suddenly pulled back and then slammed violently into a nearby a metal shelf support post.

As he falls, Graham descends to make sure he's unconscious.

A moment later, Joe, flanked by a fresh cadre of eager Special Operations soldiers, storms into the hospital:

Check the Morgue first.

As the team hustles off, Graham, still in the basement, wheels a discarded stretcher back down Katie's aisle.

Locating her again, he lifts her onto the stretcher and then moves to lay her out and disguise her as a patient. As he does, he hears footfalls and turns to see Jarvis rushing to a wall phone.

Graham is forced to abandon Katie and take off after Jarvis, who he overtakes and tackles just shy of the phone.

As they scramble for supremacy, the breaths steaming the frigid air of the morgue, Jarvis is getting the better of it with a gut-busting punch to his abdomen.

As Graham doubles over, reeling, Jarvis again rushes to the phone and grabs it to spit into it:

This is Dr. Jarvis in the morgue. I need help now!

But a blow halts Jarvis, and he keels over as Graham looks over him, holding a steel fire extinguisher.

Graham then smashes the phone off the wall, and races back to Katie.

Upstairs, the hospital quickly becomes a scene of chaos and confusion as soldiers hurry to block the exits, creating a panic among the staff and patients.

Meanwhile, as the slow-rising elevator conveys Graham and Katie back to ground-level, he touches her still drowsy face and then folds a sheet over it, as if she was dead.

In the confusion of the soldiers, staff and patients, Graham is able to push Katie's stretcher past sinister-looking soldiers who allow him to pass with a second thought.

Buoyed, Graham keeps moving.

And as he continues on, making it past several more checkpoints without incident, he begins to gain more confidence.

To his further, secret amazement, he's able to wheel Katie out of the Emergency Room door without a second look, and right up to the ambulance manned by Seal and Roan.

They quickly hop out to assist, and only then draw suspicious looks from three posted soldiers. So Seal, sensing their concern, calls to them again matter-of-factly:

Could use a hand here, mates.

Allayed by Seal's tone, they trot over to help, and together lift Katie into the back of the ambulance, still in her green bag body:

Liver donor. Gotta get her across town while she's still warm.

As the soldiers wince and gladly step back away, they hear:

Hey, what're you doin'?

All turn to see the soldiers' unit Commander hustling over:

Thought I told you guys nobody goes in or out!

Seal, Roan and Graham keep their heads down and move to climb into the ambulance as if this doesn't concern them while one of the soldiers volunteers:

We thought they were cleared.

Cleared by who?

As Graham straps into a seat belt, Seal is just opening the driver's side door when he hears:

Hold it right there!

But Seal starts to climb in anyway, pretending he didn't hear:

I said hold it right there, damn it!

Commander fires off a round to underscore his point, compelling Seal's attention. Seal turns, looking as innocently dismayed as he can:

What's the trouble, mate?

Step away from the vehicle!

Come again?

I said: step away from the vehicle. Now!

But I'm the driver, mate!

Commander levels his assault rifle at Seal.

What did I do?

Move!

If I move, mate, and we're late getting this liver donor to its new owner, two people will have died in vain tonight. Is that what you want??

Commander fires a round right past Seal's head, shattering the driver's door window.

Ya gotta be freakin' kiddin' me, brother!

But Commander clearly isn't kidding, so Seal, looking pained, takes a few steps away from the ambulance.

Inside, Graham and Roan share a worried glance as the Commander continues with Seal:

Show me some ID.

Seal's incredulolus:
Can you believe this pecker? Now he wants me to fish around for my ID while somebody's life hangs in the balance!
Now!
Seal, making a show of it, starts checking his pockets:
Think it's still in the truck, mate.
Seal tries to casually move back to the ambulance, but Commander halts him:
Don't move!
Relax, mate. Everything's going to be just fine.
Inside, Roan has seen enough. He indicates Graham should be ready to drive, and then steps out to join Seal:
What's the hell's the holdup out here?
Commander braces for an attack:
Down on your knees. Now. Both of you!
Seal scowls to Roan:
Believe this shit?
As they climb down to their knees, scoffing, Seal shoots Graham a look:
You wanna see some ID, come and get it.
Show me!
It's in my back pocket. But if I reach for it, you're going to say I was reaching for a gun. And wouldn't that just give the excuse?
Take it out!
How about you come and get it, you dickless bastard.
Commander re-grips his rifle, looking almost eager to shoot:
Now!
So Seal and Roan, timing their actions, start reaching into their back pockets. As they do, Graham slips from the passenger seat into the driver's seat.
Seal and Roan then hold up what looks to be ID badges:
Happy?
But Commander is still not happy.
Throw them over here.
If you say so.
Seal and Roan throw them over Commander's head.
He instinctively ducks and then glances back to see where they landed, at which Seal yells:
Now!
Graham stomps down on the ambulance's accelerator pedal, burning rubber out of the Emergency Room driveway, causing

Commander to wield back around and fire after him – at which Seal and Roan leap back to their feet and take off, running.

But Commander, seeing their escape attempt out of the corner of his eye, pivots back around, takes aim and fires two quick shots, dropping them both instantly.

He then wields back around to fire after the ambulance, joined by the other three soldiers.

But their shots only explode its tail-lights and lodge in its back doors as Graham veers out of range and serves back towards the city's center.

Graham races away from the scene, pounding the steering wheel at the loss of Seal and Roan, but determined to save Katie at any cost.

Barreling though the city, he swerves around a corner to speed onto the bridge, racing over the black waters.

Soon he is speeding back up the mountain highway, heading back to the lab.

He rounds the now-familiar mountain turn in the road to find the road open and clear, without any signs of a crash.

So he accelerates onwards, climbing the grade back to the tree-line, back to the source.

The facility's dark and quiet as Graham pulls into its parking area and eases into a stop. He looks around, then climbs out and moves around the back of the ambulance.

Opening its back doors, he lifts Katie into his arms, and carries as quickly as he can up to its secure entrance and balancing her in his arms, swipes her key card, which triggers its keypad and then asks for a security code.

Graham is shocked, realizing he doesn't know it.

As it blinks again, demanding an entry, Graham, guessing, mutters:

Our anniversary?

He types its date into the keypad, waits on edge, and a moment later the entrance clicks open.

Graham immediately carries her inside, and the doors lock behind him.

Barely able to see in the dim glow of the security lights, he pushes on, carrying her back to the lab, which he finally enters.

It's dark, lit only by the reflected light of the blinking diodes at the control center.

As he moves forward, angling for the tech recliners, he starts to make out a body already occupying one, and he shocks back.

Straining his eyes, edging forward again, he suddenly realizes the bodies are that of Katie and his own, lying as if in state, reclined in the chairs, wearing the High Tech glasses, suspended in Mindfall.

He staggers backwards, thunderstruck. As his mind reels, a small light clicks on. Graham whips around with Katie still in his arms to see Leo, sitting on the control panel.

Graham stares back incredulously as Leo looks up calmly as if he had been expecting Graham:

Now do you believe me?

Graham eyes him, beyond believing, and glances back at Katie and himself, lying in the tech chairs, then at the Katie cradled in his arms, and then finally back at Leo, imploring:

Believe what?

It's all nothing more than a delusion of mind.

Graham, bewildered, casts a look back at Katie and Graham lying on the recliners:

So...are they dreaming us? Or are we dreaming them?

Leo smiles:

The question is, who's dreaming all of this?

Graham's eyes burn:

All I know is I need her to live. Can you help me? Can you help her!?

Only one way now.

How!

Let go, Graham.

Let go of what?

Leo eyes him, compassionately:

Of it all. And see what remains after all your ideas, thoughts and beliefs have finally come to an end.

As Graham glares at Leo, filling with rage, he once more hears the pounding pulse of a chopper descending overhead.

Enraged, Graham charges back out of the lab with Katie in his arms and down the dark hallway to the Emergency Exit.

Making his way into the emergency exit, he again cracks open the outside door, and, picking his moment, rushes for the tree-line.

Once he's hidden in them, he looks back to see his Honda close by, apparently overlooked by the assault teams.

So, easing through the trees, Graham carries Katie right up to the parking area's edge, and, using the Humvees for cover, manages to sneak to the Honda, lifts Katie into the passenger seat, and then steals into the driver's side.

With the noise from the chopper's rotors drowning out all else, he fires up the Honda's motor, and begins easing it out of the lot…when he's spotted by the chopper's sudden brazen search beam.

Graham punches the accelerator and speeds out onto the highway, pushing the motor for all its worth.

In his side-view mirror, Graham can see the SWAT member shouting into his radio, and SWAT team rushing back to their Humvees.

As the chopper engages in aerial pursuit, Graham speeds down the winding road, trying to escape with Katie now...

But the SWAT Humvees are quickly gaining on him, and one accelerates to ram the back of the Honda, causing it to fishtail.

But Graham manages to regain control of the Honda as it speeds into a turn as bursts of automatic rifle fire strafes the Honda's hood, courtesy of a gunman in the chopper.

Graham swerves, weaves, nearly out of control just as a pair of oncoming headlights whip around the bend in the road, blinding him.

Graham is shocked as the light from the on-coming vehicle burns up into his eyes. As he raises his hand to shield his eyes, braking hard, the world – this moment – suddenly shifts into slow motion, with Graham experiencing every passing nanosecond an eternity as the Honda plows into the oncoming headlights in a crushing, shattering, exploding crash…

Graham awakens to flashing emergency lights, smoke and fire. He is lying on the road, feeling the pavement under him as someone works over him.

He looks over, dazed to see the silhouettes of paramedics performing CPR on Katie nearby. Then it all goes black.

He then comes to enough to find himself being hustled down a hospital hallway on a gurney while a team of nurses keep pace, conferring over him on the move as he loses consciousness.

Graham next opens his eyes to find himself in a hospital bed, hooked up to a network of IV's. As he looks around, wondering if this is all just another bend in Mindfall, another twisted turn, he discovers Leo and Ananda at his bedside, looking on, gravely concerned.

Ananda smiles gently as Graham looks at him, trying to understand.
You've been in a coma, Graham.
It takes Graham a beat to fathom it. Then:
How long?
Since the accident.

Graham's eyes fill with questions, so Ananda explains:
You and Katie were hit by a truck.
As Graham begins to piece it together, he suddenly panics:
Where's Katie?
Ananda takes his hand:
She...didn't make it, Graham.
Graham's mind jumbles:
You mean...in the program? In Mindfall?
Leo, getting filled with emotion, tears up as Ananda squeezes Graham's hand:
No, Graham. She died in the accident Graham, when the truck hit the Honda.
Graham stares at him, not wanting to believe it:
I'm so sorry.
But Graham continues to churn, searching for an alternative narrative:
But...what if that was all just part of it?
Part of what, Graham?
Graham looks back to Leo:
'Here' is just a delusion of mind'. Isn't that what you said?
As Leo hesitates, Graham senses another presence entering the room and looks over to see, much to his shock, Seal stepping into his hospital room; he's soon followed by Roan, and then by Ahn Li.

Graham eyes them, amazed and perplexed, only to see Saunders the Interrogator, Emily, Dr. Jarvis and Joe joining them, followed by the various soldiers Graham battled with, then the thug, and finally Bill and Judy – all together, all gazing at him, regarding him with a wordless knowing, an unspoken comprehension.

Ananda and Leo, noting Graham's sudden preoccupation, turn to see what Graham's looking at, but see only the hospital room's walls.

But Graham continues to eye them all, feeling a peace descend on him, surround him, and emerge from within him to cradle him like a new mother.

Everything in Graham wants to join with them, to somehow thank them as their faces glow at him. But as he endeavors to get out of bed, his visitors suddenly begin to vibrate, shimmering into blue shadows which suddenly lift away, one by one, disappearing into the ceiling...angels all.
Graham?
He looks back to find Ananda searching his eyes:
Is there anything you need?

Graham's face fills with a new appreciation, a new, growing realization that all of it, all Katie had ever endeavored to awaken in him, was to prepare him for this moment.

As his eyes fill with this new understanding, this new awareness for the purpose of it all, the EKG's alarm suddenly blares to life.

Ananda immediately tries to call for help, but Graham grips his hand all the more, keeping close.

So Leo goes for help as Graham continues to slip away.

A moment later, an emergency response team rushes in, pushing a defibrillator cart as they force Ananda and Leo aside, breaking Graham's grip on Ananda just as Graham flat-lines, triggering more alarms.

Ananda and Leo look on as the team hurries through its paces, administering a series of increasingly intense defibrillator jolts to Graham's chest, shocking his body.

As they work, Graham's eyes gaze up vacantly as if this was all happening to someone else, somewhere else.

He then slowly closes his eyes and, as gentle as a breeze, slips away as the light dims and the room's din fades, releasing him into silence. A stillness. A womb.

But then a breeze rises up, brushing against his skin and tussling his hair. And Graham's restful eyes flicker open to discover a blue-hued twilight.

Above him a dark sky stirs with dark clouds.

Around him a vast, desolate Salt Flats stretches out to a dark horizon.

As he recognizes this moment, he feels a sudden rush of old fears fill him.

He quickly climbs to his feet to peer out into the darkness, seeing again the black ribbon of the tidal wave riding the horizon, rolling impossibly over the plain, devouring the world.

Gripped by terror, he turns once more to run, only to suddenly see Katie standing calmly behind him as if she had always been there.

He rushes to her, trying to warn her, but she simply smiles.

So he grabs her, trying to pull into a run, but she resists him, pulling him back into her arms to hold him, to comfort him, to reassure him as the breeze kicks up into a bracing wind and thunder booms, flashing crackling forks of lightning.

Graham tries once more to escape, to save them, but Katie holds him firm, unmoved.

And slowly, despite his every instinct to flee, he feels himself succumbing to her embrace, releasing himself into her calm, allowing her love as well as his fear to fill him, to penetrate and finally purge him.

She then gently turns his face to the monumental wave as rampages towards them, rising up as big as the sky to dwarf them, arcing, it seems, all the way to heaven as it readies to crush, subsume and annihilate, along with everything in its path, when…

When it suddenly begins to melt away as if being absorbed into the earth, its cresting waters quickly receding, diminishing before Graham's amazed eyes as it collapses before them, dying away in moments to create a new and glistening sea before them, arriving finally at their feet in a gently lapping wave of foam.

Katie turns her gentle gaze to him, and takes his hand.

Step by step, she leads him. And as they walk out onto its delicate waters, a new awareness opens to him like the dark skies above, revealing an infinite consciousness of welcoming stars, embracing them like long-lost loves finally come home.

There's so much more than mind, my love. So much more.

About the Author

~*~

Raised in Los Angeles, Darryl Sollerh's recent works include "SHaDOW GAME", a Readers' Views FIRST PLACE AWARD winner, as well as "ALIBIS OF THE HEART", "EDDY FALLS", "TRANCER" and "COWBOY AND INDIAN", a Readers' Favorite SILVER MEDAL AWARD winner. All are available in print, as well as on iPad, Kindle, Nook and eReaders everywhere. For more, visit www.DarrylSollerh.com.

~*~

In loving memory of

Dr. Harvey Mindess

~*~

www.ingramcontent.com/pod-product-compliance
Lightning Source LLC
Chambersburg PA
CBHW020640130626
46552CB00003B/1329